KU-441-417

Hard Cash

HARD CASH
Derek Smith

faber and faber
LONDON · BOSTON

First published in Great Britain in 1991
by Faber and Faber Limited
3 Queen Square London WC1N 3AU

Photoset by Input Typesetting Ltd, Wimbledon
Printed in Great Britain by Clays Ltd, St Ives plc

© Derek Smith, 1991

Derek Smith is hereby identified as the author of this work in accordance
with Section 77 of the Copyright, Design and Patents Act 1988.

A CIP record for this book is available from the British Library.

ISBN: 0–571–16174–X

To Marva, Thomas and Rebecca

1

Warby asked me to write it down. He said I was the one who was good at that sort of thing and he was sick of people saying things that just weren't true. As for me – I just want to get it out. There's a lot of talk anyway – so they might as well hear how it was rather than a load of lies.

I've been saying all that because I'm trying to work out where to begin. How much you want to know. Whether I should say what we look like and describe our houses and things. Though I'm not much good at describing things and it'll probably bore you as much reading it as it will bore me writing it.

Myself I like adventure; especially space stories – strange planets and far galaxies. I like it to move so that you can't put it down, you want to know so badly what happens next.

So I'd better jump in. I'll fill in the other bits as we get to it. There was this derelict building on Chrisp Street. It wasn't the only derelict building – there were half a dozen of them in a row, all tinned up. Doors, windows – no glass, just corrugated iron. The yards were full of rubbish. Old armchairs, black bags full of rotting rubbish, mattresses, a broken washing machine. You know the sort of stuff that gets dumped.

This house had the corrugated iron over the door loose. Not very loose, a bit loose. And then Warby encouraged it. He's never one to hold back and he can be a bit silly. Like when he made faces at those big kids and got himself beat up. Dancing up and down, 'Can't catch me'. Well they could alright and they did alright. You think maybe he would learn but I don't think he ever will.

Don't get me wrong, I like Warby. Even now he's my best mate. Warby – well he's a bit wild. But he likes doing things – that's what I like about him. You suggest something, he doesn't bring you down but says 'Yes, OK' or 'Why not'. I don't make friends that easy. I find it hard to talk to people, till I get to know someone that is, but Warby when we first moved into the flats, he just came up and asked if I'd like to see his lizards. Warby's great like that, but what makes him great also makes him stupid at times and that's what this story is really about.

Now you know about Warby, I'd better tell you about me. Shorty they call me. Shorty Roberts. I hate the name, my real name's David – but no one except my mum and sister call me it.

I don't know whether I'm going to be a good story-teller if I can't stick to the story and tell you about what I think all the time. But then it's no good just saying this happened and this happened if you don't know who it happened to. I think I'll get better as I get into it.

2

Anyway it was one dinner-time during term time and like most days we'd just gone off. My mum thought I had school dinners but I used to go off with Warby and spend our dinner money. Sometimes we'd pool it and have a few sweets, some fruit, a drink, things like that. Another time one of us would go off and we'd have to surprise the other. I remember the time Warby came back with two pomegranates and a coconut. We spent the whole of the dinner-time trying to crack it.

We were heading for the railway. We'd climb over the wall and there was this derelict signal box. We'd put a padlock on the door and we used to use it as a sort of clubhouse. One of us would get the grub and the other wait at HQ. On this day Warby spotted the loose bit of tin.

We'd been passing those houses ever since we'd started at Kier Hardie School, nearly nine months ago. Every window and door of those houses was covered with corrugated iron, like it was stitched on. I used to wonder what it was like inside; pitch black pretty obviously, but what had been left behind. But up to now it would have been easier to get into a tin of sardines with a lolly stick.

Now this corner was stuck up like a dog-eared page. Warby began to pull at it. Chrisp Street's not that busy but it's just off the market and people are always coming by. I could see an old lady pushing her shopping basket on wheels. 'Someone coming,' I called out. But Warby had already disappeared in the house.

How would it'd have turned out if I'd have left him. Maybe alright. Warby always acts up more when

3

there's people watching – and I suspect if I had left him in the house he'd have come out pretty soon. Anyway that didn't happen.

I let the old lady go. She gave me a funny look as I was standing there. A strange place to stand. You wouldn't wait for anyone there and there wasn't anything to look at. She crossed the road and then looked back at me. I dipped down and tied me shoelace up, slowly just to do something. Then she was gone.

And I went in the hole that Warby had made.

It was dark inside, the only light behind me. There was a damp smell like old rags and a smell of dust. I didn't move for a bit getting used to the light. I was in a hallway with two doors on either side and a staircase a little way in and beyond that more hallway and from then on it was too dark to see.

I opened the first door next to me and peered in. I couldn't see anything – it was pitch apart from a chink of light above a window. I stepped into the room, and fell astride a rafter. There were no floorboards!

I'd hurt meself a bit. And as I lifted myself up I heard a rip. I put my hand to my trousers and felt the hole I'd torn in my backside.

I cursed at Warby and went back out into the hallway. There was a banging coming from upstairs. What was he doing up there? Blooming nutter.

What would Mum say about the tear in my trousers? More banging upstairs. Carefully I made my way along the hallway, feeling the floor with a toe before putting my foot down.

The stairs had no bannisters. I couldn't see them at

4

all and just climbed by feel, wondering all the time what was holding them up. Then I put my foot out and there was nothing there. I knelt down and felt in front with my hands. There wasn't a landing.

'Warby,' I called, in a hushed shout. The house was a total booby trap and I was feeling in need of company.

The door ahead of me opened and spilled out light from the room. There was Warby in the light of a sky-light smiling in a peculiar way. Over Warby's shoulder was a sledgehammer.

'Where'd you get that?' I said.

'Just lying about. Come across.'

I could see the gap clearly now, between me and him. It was about four feet across.

'You must be joking.'

'Just a quick step,' said Warby, still smiling at me, his nose turned up in that superior way he has when he knows something you don't. I looked down, I looked at him.

'It's not as far as it looks,' he said.

'What you doing?' I asked.

'Bit of demolition. See what I done. We can go right across the roofs.'

The gap seemed awfully wide. There wasn't even room for any run up. I leaned back on the landing wall, bracing myself, taking deep breaths. In out, in out. I sucked in a final breath and leaped.

I made it. Or at least thought I did for a second. Then the bit of floor I landed on cracked and gave way. I fell through.

Down to the ground floor I fell. Cracked through the

floorboards and went through again. When I struck ground I was completely winded, lying on my back and unable to even shout out.

I could hear Warby running down the stairs.

The space I was in was dark, the only light from the hole I had fallen through, up which I could see the hole in the landing where I had tried my jump. I felt like a cat looking up a well.

Warby had arrived on the floor above and crouched down and peered at me.

'You alright?'

In reply my throat rasped like a bunged-up vacuum cleaner. I didn't know whether I was alright.

2

'Hey Shorty,' he called again anxiously, 'you alright?'

The outline of his head stood out against the jagged rim of the hole like a skull on a ring.

I tried to say something but all that came out was a breathy squeal. A ton weight seemed to be pressing down on my chest.

'Your eyes are open,' said Warby. 'That's a good sign.'

Good for who? My neck could be broken, that wouldn't affect my eyes. I could be totally paralysed except my eyes could move from side to side. Everything in me could be dead but for my eyes (I don't know if that's possible).

I wanted to say something, to indicate that I was at least alive. I tried to call again.

'Hang about,' said Warby, 'I'll see what I can find.'

His head disappeared and I could hear him walking about above me. Now I began to really worry about myself. I knew I wasn't dead. I didn't know whether I had broken my neck, my back or any one or more of the 600-odd bones in the human body. Maybe I would have to spend my life in a wheelchair being pushed about. And I remembered those blokes I'd seen in the London marathon speeding along in their wheelchairs. They seemed pretty cheerful so it couldn't be as bad as you might think. Though it must be difficult going to bed or to the toilet.

Maybe I was even worse. What if I'd broken my neck? I'd seen a picture of a man with a broken neck. He lay on a bed with his head sideways and saw everyone through a mirror. He read books through a mirror, watched tele through a mirror. He was able to work a computer with his tongue so he could write letters. He said the worst thing was being fed.

When I thought of that, being fed for the rest of my life, tears came to my eyes. This should be Warby! He had goaded me, he should be lying here with his neck broken, Warby should be the one to be fed all his life. Not me.

A floorboard began to come through the hole. It stopped on the floor beside me, the top resting against the edge of the hole. Warby was standing there and lowering a second plank.

'Be with you in a minute,' he shouted down.

He placed the second plank next to the first. Then holding onto the top of the planks, he let his legs down the boards, and like a giant four-legged thing began to walk down backwards.

On his knees beside me, Warby put his hand over my mouth. 'You're breathing alright.' He then began to feel my neck, to squeeze it.

'Stop it,' I croaked.

'I heard that,' shouted Warby and lifted me to a

seated position. My chest was hurting but my head was definitely staying on my neck and when he let go my back seemed to be supporting me.

Without warning Warby began to thump me on the back. Over and over. I began to splutter and choke. And then to cough. Tears had again welled up in my eyes.

'You trying to kill me,' I said almost normally.

'You're alright,' said Warby, and I could see from the way he was staring at me and the grin breaking out on his face that he had been really worried. My voice was returning, my chest hurt, but movement was returning to my neck and arms. Now I'd never know what it was like to spend my life in a wheelchair or write a letter with my tongue.

'How we going to get up?' said Warby. I hadn't got that far but looking up the planks – yes the slope did seem rather steep.

'Let's have a look,' said Warby, and he began to walk around in the cellar. He disappeared in the far gloom. I could hear his footsteps padding about and his complaints about the smell.

'There's something here,' he called. 'It's heavy.' I could hear him straining and swearing. 'Flippin' heavy. Must be full of bricks.'

He appeared out of the darkness pushing in front of him a long box. It bulldozed a wave of soil as it came. When he reached me, he stopped and sat down on the box exhausted.

I dragged myself up. Standing rather shakily I began

to twist my neck round and round and rub my chest which was still aching.

'S'a toolbox,' said Warby. 'We stand it on end. And we should be able to pull ourselves through.'

He put his hand through the handle at one end, and with great effort heaved it onto the other end. With his tongue hanging out like a thirsty dog he stood there getting his strength back. Warby always acts out he's worse than he is. Recovering, he climbed onto the box. His head just came through the hole.

'See,' he called in triumph and jumped down, knocking the box over. It opened and the contents spilled out. Warby crouched down to look.

'Blimey.'

I came over. Warby was holding a bundle of bank notes.

3

Warby threw a bundle of notes at me. I ducked. Warby began to pelt me. I covered my face with my hands and he stopped. I uncovered my face and there he was waiting. He began to rain them on me again. It was a very one-sided fight. I was still recovering while Warby was jumping up and down like an ape that had just discovered bananas.

I scuttled around the room, trying to get out of the way. He followed me, throwing bundles. Every time I looked up, a fresh one would hit me on the face. I would turn round, they would hit me on the back, and then Warby would dart in front of me and begin afresh.

'Pack it in,' I screamed.

Warby kept pelting. I lay on the ground and pulled my head into my chest armadillo fashion. The pelting went on with short pauses which I imagined was Warby going back to the box for more.

Suddenly I had absolutely enough. I jumped up and began to throw them back as hard as I could. Now it was Warby's turn to run, wherever he ran I followed throwing. Finally I got him in a corner.

'Fainlights,' he said crossing his fingers.

I grabbed his leg, pulled him to the ground and sat on his chest. There is a point when my temper cracks. Then I don't care what's coming at me, I just go for it. Now I thumped up and down on Warby.

I stopped. 'You gonna say sorry?'

He gave me a sour look. I gave him a thump.

'Alright, Shorty, I'm sorry.'

I gave him another thump. 'You gonna pick 'em up?'

He nodded. I got off.

Warby got up and brushed himself down. 'We gotta have a talk,' he said.

I glared at him. He began picking up the bundles. 'We've got to get that money out of here and decide what to do with it.'

'It'll take half an hour to tidy up,' I moaned. 'And then how we going to get it out?'

Warby looked at the box. He looked at the planks. That just didn't look possible.

'I'll go over the market and get some bags,' he said. 'You collect it all up.'

He stood up on the box and began to climb out. I grabbed him by the waist and pulled him off. 'You tidy up, I'll get the bags.' I climbed on the box. Warby grabbed me by the foot and I had to hop off. Warby jumped on, I grabbed his foot.

Warby sighed like he was picking up a rattle for a baby for the umpteenth time.

'Shorty.' His tone halted me. 'Whoever left that money is going to come back for it.'

Warby went off to get the bags. I went through the cellar collecting all the bundles. Where it was dark I got on hands and knees and just scrabbled about, feeling for them. After a while I couldn't see any and I couldn't feel any. I had them all in a pile by the box.

Bit by bit I transferred them from the cellar to the hallway above. When it was all done I climbed up and waited for Warby.

He came back with two dustbin bags.

We bundled the money into the sacks, took one each and went to the front door. Warby climbed out first without a sack. In a few moments he gave the all clear. I passed out the sacks and came out after.

We trundled off down the road like a couple of gnomes, each with our grey sack. When there was no one about we ran, whenever we saw anyone we stopped running and tried to look innocent. Warby though always looks guilty. He was whistling in a funny way, stretching his neck forward like an ostrich. Trying so hard not to be noticed you'd think everyone was bound to.

Finally we got to the railway bridge, crossed it quickly, and climbed the wall.

Our hut is just over the wall. It's a boarded-up signal box at the top of the railway cutting. You can hardly see it for the boards over the windows. Though it's hard to see why they bothered as they must've stripped everything out when they left. Maybe they thought they would use it again one day. The cutting is between two tunnels maybe a hundred yards apart. One of them is hardly a tunnel, more like a wide bridge. The other one is long, so long you can't see the end.

There's no light in the hut so we use candles. We

13

fixed up a little shelf in the middle of one wall, just over head height and on it we put a saucer with the candle. It makes it gloomy in there but we like it like that. The only furniture is three beer crates we borrowed. Two we use for seats and one for a table.

'Let's count it,' said Warby.

First we counted how much was in each bundle. There were fifty £20 notes in each, making £1,000. Then I counted how many bundles I had and Warby did the same for his sackful.

Finally we had finished. 'How many you got, Warby?' I asked.

'You first,' he said.

'I asked first.'

Warby had his stubborn look. I tried to see how many bundles he had. He covered them with his sack. I covered mine. We sat looking at each other like book ends.

Finally Warby said, 'Let's have a game.'

'What?'

'Gambling.'

'We can play heads or tails,' I said.

I explained the game. We each toss a coin and then cover it. Then we had to guess how many heads or tails. Like it could be two heads, a head and a tail, or two tails.

So we both put £1,000 in the pot. We tossed and put the coins down on the beer-crate table.

'Two heads,' said Warby.

'A head and a tail,' I said.

Then we lifted up one at a time and I won £2,000.

We carried on. When no one won we just increased the pot and did it again until someone did. I won most because I knew something Warby didn't.

I'm quite good at maths and I got this book as a prize, called *Mathematical Tricks*. Anyway it had this section on heads and tails. And I knew that with two coins there are four possible ways it could come up – not just three. That's because a head and a tail can come up as head and tail or as a tail and a head. So I just stuck to a head and a tail. Chucked in two heads or two tails occasionally so I didn't look too obvious . . .

After about forty minutes I had won £39,000. Warby was getting ratty. So I explained – which was pretty stupid of me because Warby blew the candle out – and said he wasn't going to relight it unless I gave the money back.

I agreed. Warby relit the candle.

'We are going to return it, aren't we?' I said.

Warby hooted and chucked half a dozen bundles up in the air. 'Finders keepers.'

'It must be stolen,' I said.

'Not necessarily.'

'Who'd leave their money in an empty house?'

'Maybe some rich person. They used to live there and when they left they forgot they had this money in the cellar.'

'The money's new,' I said, 'and those houses have been empty for years.'

That quietened Warby. I could see though he was still trying to outsmart me. He had his thinking frown.

'Either someone stole it,' I said, 'or we just have.'

'Not necessarily.'

'What then?'

He didn't answer but kept frowning.

'We should return it,' I said.

'Look,' said Warby, 'no one saw us go in, right? No one saw us go out, right? So no one knows we've got it, right?'

'Yes,' I agreed reluctantly.

'What would you like?' said Warby. 'More than anything.'

'A telescope,' I said without having to think.

'You could have a hundred.'

'Maybe we could give some back?' I suggested meekly.

'Come off it. They'll want to know where the rest is.'

'I wonder how much there is.'

We each said how much we'd counted and I added it up. 'It's £246,000.'

'What's that divided by two?' said Warby.

I worked it out, '£123,000.'

4

We divided the money into two and Warby began building a pyramid. He started with a square base one bundle thick. Then built on it, making the next one a bit smaller. He carried on until he ran out of notes. There was still a chunk cut off the top.

'Lend us 20,000 quid.' He grinned.

'I'm a bit short this week,' I said.

'Don't be tight. I need a new car. Last one ran out of petrol.'

While he was building I'd been thinking about a twelve-inch reflector telescope I'd seen. Motorized so it turns at the same speed as the earth. You need that if you take photos, otherwise you just get light tracks.

Night after night I would search the same section of the sky, taking hundreds of photos. Then one night I would find a star that moved across the star background. I would check through my photos. Yes there it was moving night after night. I had discovered the tenth planet in the solar system. Planet David!

'You know what I'd get?' said Warby.

'No,' reluctantly leaving my own dream.

He gave a secret smile. 'A panther.'

Warby is mad on animals. He's got hamsters, fish and salamanders. A panther was definitely a step up.

Trying not to act surprised – I didn't want to sound like a teacher – I said, 'Where would you keep it?'

'In a zoo.' His face was dreamy and soft. He could see that panther. Was he feeding it? Or maybe in the cage with it, wrestling with it? Then he added, in a quiet voice as if it wasn't really for me to hear, 'My zoo.'

I shook my head. 'It's too much, Warby. We've got to give it back.'

'No!' He stood up. His eyes were blazing.

'Then I'll give my half back,' I said.

'You do that and they'll come for mine.'

'I won't tell them a thing.'

He kicked the box he'd been sitting on. 'How can I believe that?'

'Alright,' I said with a sigh, 'I'll give it all to you.'

Warby looked at me in disbelief. 'You'd give me all that?'

'Yes.'

Warby became silent. I watched him carefully. I didn't really know whether I would give it all to him. I had said that without thinking. Warby sat down again and began playing with his pyramid of bank notes. Slowly he took it apart, piling them in careful heaps of £1,000. Each bundle he caressed, sniffing it, rubbing it against his face before putting it on the heap. By the light of the flickering candle as he bent over the money I felt I was seeing him in fifty years' time. There would be Warby working late in the bank, everyone gone, hair long at the back and bald at the front, wire glasses perched on his nose, counting the last note.

'Oh come on, Shorty,' he looked up at me. 'Just think what we can do with it. We'll be really careful. I won't spend anything without talking to you first. In fact how about we both have to agree before a penny gets spent on anything?'

'That's a good idea,' I said.

'So we keep it?'

'Not me.'

'Just think about it.' He was standing over me. I could see panthers in his eyes, long cages and big cats, and Warby with a whip and a chair. 'Think about it tonight. Then we talk about it tomorrow dinner-time? Yeh?'

'There's no point . . .'

'Please.' There were tears in his eyes. I hesitated. Warby is my best friend.

'Alright. Tomorrow dinner-time.'

I knew it wouldn't be any easier then.

5

By the time I arrived back at the flats the sun had already gone behind our block. The shadow lay across the gravel, over the roofs of the pram sheds, and half-way up the block opposite.

All the blocks on the estate are the same. There's fifteen altogether, five stories high; dirty red-brick buildings, stairs at either end and balconies running along the front. I never saw a pram in the pram sheds, not a whole one that is. Most of the doors are smashed in.

What tells you most about our estate is the number of empties. It hit me when we first moved in, when we climbed out the van – maybe a quarter were boarded up. I remember thinking – nobody wants to live here. My mum was trying hard not to cry.

Everyone's on the transfer list. Sounds like a fourth division football team, except more like tenth division. The insides are not bad, they've got bathrooms, and they're not damp or anything – but it's the outside that gets you. You think how did this ever get built? Was some architect proud of this once?

My mum had one choice – this or nothing. We spent

three months in the battered women's hostel and Mum was in a state. She's very clean and it was impossible there with everyone on top of each other.

Before that we had a flat in North London. On a new estate; a hundred times better than this place. Central heating, only two floors, even a little garden. We had to leave it to get away from my dad.

It was the night he attacked Kathy, my sister, with a hammer that done it. My mum I reckon would've stood it if it was just her. He's broken her arm, given her black eyes, stitches. One time she spent two weeks in hospital and lost a kid – but she stood it. She loved him she said cuz he was a rough 'un. She thought he would protect her from anything. My poor mum. She's soft, she tries to hide it but you can always tell that she's upset. This place kills her. She won't even have our relatives over. We have to go and see them. Even though Uncle Bob and Uncle Jeff have got cars.

When I got home Kathy and my mum were sitting at the kitchen table, having a cup of tea. Mum was smoking.

Kathy said, 'Mr Kershaw's bin asking about you.'

'Where you been?' said Mum.

'Nowhere much.' I slinked into the kitchen cabinets.

'He's bin with that Peter Warburton,' said Kathy.

'Shut up,' I said.

My mum said quietly, 'Don't shout at your sister.'

I looked up for an instant and caught my sister's stern face. She's only a year older than me but you'd think she was twenty.

'Look at his trousers,' said Kathy.

'Turn round,' said my mum. I did so. 'How could you?' she said. 'You've only had them three weeks.'

'Sorry,' I mumbled.

'Sorry, sorry, I'll give you sorry.' She rose quickly and struck me twice on the seat with the flat of her hand. I pulled away. It hadn't hurt that much, her tone hurt me more.

'Do you think I'm made of money? Do you both think I'm made of money? Do you know how long it takes me to earn enough for a pair of trousers?' She spat the words at me. 'A day! A whole day's work. Can't you grow out of them like other kids?'

I stood against the draining board, gripping the edge, waiting for her to wind down.

'How are we going to manage? Your sister's broken her sandals. She wants to go on a school trip to Germany.'

Kathy was now looking into her teacup, picking the crumbs on the table.

'Are the two of you going to pay this?' Mum picked a bill off the table and handed it to me. 'Go on. Read it. Then tell me who is going to pay it?'

It was a gas bill for £98.

Suddenly Mum was crying. She covered her eyes with one hand and sobbed.

'Don't cry, Mum,' said Kathy. 'I'll wear my plimsoles.'

'Oh God, oh God, oh God,' she sobbed over and over. I wanted to say something but felt I had caused all this. My bunking off, my trousers. And you never knew with adults when they might turn on you again.

She was wiping her eyes with the tips of her fingers. 'Take them off and bring me my sewing basket.'

While she was sewing my trousers I went to my room. The only other pair I had was in the wash. I put my coat on and lay on the bed. She wanted £100 and I had more than a hundred thousand. And I wanted to give it back! Here I lived on a dump estate – and I wanted to give it back!

Two pairs of trousers, one pair of shoes. I wanted to cry too. For the things we never did, for the things we couldn't do. For my dad, who I hated and who I used to dream would turn up with arms full of presents. We used to have money, we used to be alright. Why couldn't I have been born to rich parents?

Kathy came in with my trousers.

'Mr Kershaw gave me a note. You're for it tomorrow.'

I was dressed now. 'Do you have to tell on me?'

She stuck out her tongue. 'Do you have to bunk off? Anyway it was all in the note.' And she left the room.

I don't like Kathy. She's a year older and she can run faster. She can also fight me, although she fights dirty. Dad liked her better, and Mum is always telling people how pretty she is. I don't think she's pretty. She's plump and I think a pig's tail should be on a pig's bum. Her friends are a pretty giggly bunch and they all like Warby.

And I knew if I were rich – they'd like me too.

6

I go to school with Warby and this morning I had some talking to do with him. I rushed down the stairs. When I got to the bottom I tripped over a green double mattress, lying in the lobby like a flat caterpillar, with white stuffing coming out. Annoyed, I picked myself up. They'd thrown it right across the stairs. I pulled it away. Outside I met Warby.

On the road running by the flats cars were backed up bumper to bumper on one side of the road. In the evening they would be backed up on the other.

Me and Warby got a kick out of walking past them. There they were red-faced, hunched over their wheels, one per car, like angry hedgehogs. Every morning and evening out they came, God knows where to or from. I used to think maybe the town hall people that built this place were in those cars. Maybe they felt guilty – but I doubt it. All they felt was annoyed that the road wasn't wider.

Warby was broody. I knew he was working up to something but I thought I'd let it come out in its own time. At last he said, 'I bin thinking.' He paused to let me know it was important, then added, 'Maybe you're right.'

'Eh?'

'About the money.'

'What d'you mean?'

'Giving it back. Maybe you're right. It's too much for a couple of kids.'

This was not what I was expecting. I had dreamed all night of money. I had lain awake listing the things I would buy. I had seen the love and gratitude of my mother. My sister had begged for some . . . And now Warby wanted to back out!

There was a shout from behind. It was Jimmy.

'Shut up for now,' said Warby. 'Talk about it at break.'

Jimmy joined us and began talking about a TV programme neither of us had seen. I wasn't listening, a vision of the signal box with its door swinging had taken over me.

I tapped Warby on the shoulder. 'Do you think it's still there?'

'What?' said Jimmy.

Warby started, then said, 'Course it is.'

'We should've moved it,' I said.

'Where?'

Jimmy said, 'What you two talking about?'

We ignored him. I said with an air of desperation, 'I've changed my mind. What I said yesterday, I don't want that.'

Warby stopped. I stopped. His face was serious, his

eyes searching mine. 'How do I know you won't change it again?'

I stuck a finger in my mouth and took it out. I said, 'See this wet, see this dry, cut my throat if I tell a lie.'

He spat on his hand. I spat on mine. 'Shake,' he said.

Our wet hands squeezed each other. Warby said, 'If I lie and do you wrong, May the devil slit my tongue.'

He spat on his other hand. I spat on mine. We now shook both hands.

I said, 'Kill my sister, kill my mother, If I should tell another.'

We shook both hands seesaw fashion and then separated.

Jimmy said, 'Can I be in?'

Warby laughed and shoved me on the shoulder, winking as he did so. 'Friday fool,' he said.

'Who?' said Jimmy.

'You. There's nothing to be in on.'

Jimmy's face grew sulky. 'I don't believe you.'

'More fool you.'

We teased him the rest of the way to school.

7

We had science for the first two periods. Normally I like science. I like to know how things work. But today I couldn't listen. Half of me was making plans what to do with the money. I would send big kids off with fivers to run errands. I would say who wants a milk shake and treat the street. I would hire the swimming pool for the week. I would take a taxi to the Planetarium and leave it waiting outside. I would go into a toy shop followed by the shop assistant with a note pad. I would just touch things and say, 'Deliver it.'

But every dream was interrupted by the open signal box door. It kept coming through like one of those commercials that make you sick because they do them over and over. My guts ached with the thought of it. I didn't hear a word of the lesson or take any notice of anyone around me. I just wanted to run out of the school, across the market, up the road, and over the footbridge. I just wanted to know it hadn't happened.

Someone was prodding me on the elbow. I looked up and a note was passed to me. It said, 'Do what I do. W.'

I looked over to Warby and gave him the thumbs up.

I didn't know what he meant but knew he felt the same as I did.

He put his hand up. 'Please miss, I feel sick.' He had gone to the front of the class and was talking quietly to Miss Stewart. I couldn't tell her I felt sick too. That would never wash. Or would it?

Suddenly I was walking down the aisle.

'I feel sick too, Miss.'

She gave me a stern look through her gold-rimmed spectacles. I tried to look as miserable as possible. I rubbed my stomach which was really aching.

Warby said, 'It must've been the pie, Miss. We both had some . . . for breakfast.'

'I didn't know you ate together,' said Miss Stewart.

'Yes, Miss,' said Warby, 'Shorty's mum goes to work early and . . . ' He stopped, held his stomach and began to moan.

Miss Stewart hesitated. If we were really ill and she ignored us she'd be for it. I know that because a teacher in my junior school got sued for keeping a deaf girl in.

Warby was doing a real performance. Rolling his head around, rubbing his stomach, doubling over. I began to feel left out so I began to moan and act up a bit. Miss Stewart was lost for words, her mouth was opening and closing like a puzzled goldfish. At last she said, 'Go for a walk round the playground – and I'll be along in a few minutes.'

We headed for the door. Jimmy shouted out, 'They're alright Miss.' I found it hard to keep from laughing. We got out quickly. Just as the door closed I heard Jimmy shout, 'Friday fool!'

In the corridor we did start laughing. Not loudly, but giggling as we made for the playground. We had certainly fooled Miss Stewart. She was probably going for a second opinion but we weren't going to stick around long enough to get one. We kept looking behind us to make sure she wasn't following. As we went through the swing doors we bumped into Mr Kershaw.

'Just the two I'm looking for,' he said. 'Wait for me outside my study.'

We sat in two chairs outside his room wondering what we were in for. The long corridor was empty except for the two of us. Outside girls were playing netball and those left over running round skittles. It occurred to me even now to run for it – and sort it out later.

'What's he want us for?' asked Warby.

I remembered the letter that Kathy had brought home. 'It's about bunking off yesterday.'

'Just say you won't do it again.'

'I want to do it right now.'

Warby smiled. 'I made a list of all the things I want.'

'If it's gone that's all you'll have.'

Mr Kershaw was coming along the corridor with Miss Stewart. I bit my lip, it was all falling to bits. Warby was again looking sick, slumped in the chair, rubbing his stomach and moaning. I thought what's the point they don't believe us.

He stood over us. His face was pink and shiny, his white hair very white. I glimpsed his fingernails, trimmed and very clean – it didn't seem possible to have them so clean.

'I'll deal with them now, Miss Stewart.'

She looked at us both and frowned. 'I hope it's not catching,' she said and turned on her heels.

'So,' said Mr Kershaw, 'you're sick are you?'

We both mumbled, 'Yes sir.'

'Piece of pie for breakfast?'

'Yes sir,' said Warby.

'So you have breakfast at his place do you?' he said to me.

'Yes sir.'

'And your sister? Does she?'

That hit me like a hard snowball. I knew what he was going to do now – ask her. And even if she was on my side she wouldn't know what to say.

'It's not a proper breakfast,' said Warby. 'He just has a bite while he waits for me.'

'Shall I phone your mother?'

'We're not on the phone,' said Warby.

'Come inside,' he said to Warby and to me, 'you stay here.'

They went into the study. I wished I'd gone in first. At least Warby knew what he was getting. I've only sat here a couple of times before. Once I hadn't done anything, I was just there to collect a paper. It didn't make any difference. I still felt a criminal. Mr Kershaw asked me what I'd done. And I answered nothing. Nothing sir, he said. They have this way of putting you in the wrong.

Mr Kershaw came out in front of Warby. He told Warby to sit down and me to go in. I glanced quickly at Warby, he mouthed something – I couldn't make it out. Then I was in the room.

It's a long room with a desk at one end, and shelves all round it full of files. By the side of the desk was a calendar with a picture of two kids in a canoe in bright orange life jackets. One of the dates had a circle round. I wondered what it was. Something schoolish. You couldn't imagine Mr Kershaw circling a birthday or anything normal.

He stood over me. I could smell soap. 'What sort of pie did you have for breakfast?'

And I knew he had asked Warby exactly the same question. Meat pie I thought, but no you wouldn't have that for breakfast.

'You must know what sort of pie it was.'

I had to say something. Then in an instant Warby's lips made sense.

'Apple pie.'

Mr Kershaw smiled. 'With or without cloves?'

'What's cloves, sir?'

'Never mind.' He paced around a little. 'Why do you think your colleague said it was meat pie?'

'Don't know, sir.'

'If two people are asked what pie they eat and one says it's apple pie and the other says it's meat – what would you think?'

'That it wasn't very well cooked, sir.'

Mr Kershaw laughed. He went to the door and brought Warby in.

'I'm sending you both off to the health centre and I want you to come straight back.'

8

We were running. I said to Warby, 'What pie did you say?'

'Apple,' he called as he pulled ahead of me across the market.

The market was busy, lots of stalls and lots of shoppers, mostly women, some with toddlers in pushchairs. Bustle and busy. Fruit stalls, vegetables, knick knacks, clothes and everything. Warby disappeared into them. I decided not to follow but to take the long way round. I figured I could beat him with Warby having to fight his way through shoppers. I sprinted along the top and turned down the side and went sprawling into a woman with two shopping bags.

She fell over backwards and so did I. All the vegetables came out of one of her bags.

'You bloody fool,' she screamed at me. 'Can't you see where you're going?'

I helped her up. She was wearing jeans and a waistcoat. Looked quite young, but her hair was going grey. I ran around picking vegetables up, saying sorry a hundred times.

Calming down she said, 'Why you in such a rush? You just won the pools?'

'My mum's having a baby.'

'It won't help her much if you get knocked down by a car.'

I said sorry for the last time and carried on my way. Warby was at the corner of the market waiting for me.

'Come on,' he said and began to run.

I called after him, 'I'm walking.'

Warby ran on. I walked as fast as I could. I was now passing the tinned-up building. There was a red car outside the house we'd gone into. A thin-faced man in a lumberjacket and cap was leaning on the car and picking his fingernails. I looked at the door of the house. The gap in the corrugated iron was much larger.

'Whatd'you want?' said the man.

'Nothing.'

'Clear off then.' His thin face had gone nasty.

I ran. And stopped at the railway bridge. From its wall I carefully looked back. The man was still there, picking his nails.

I knew he was on lookout. He had friends in the house and it was obvious what they were doing. I stayed in my position. Every so often the man glanced up and down the street. Suddenly he whistled. Two men in overalls ran out of the house.

I could now hear excited raised voices. The man on the car started to push at one of the men in overalls who suddenly drew back his fist. They now sparred around each other until the third man came between. They stopped circling. Conversation grew heated again and then calmed. Finally the first man looked up and down the street and all three disappeared into the house.

When I got to the signal box Warby greeted me with a smile.

'It's all there,' he said.

I told him what I had just seen.

'They're after the money,' he said.

I nodded, a little annoyed that he had said the obvious.

'We've got to move it.' Warby was saying all the things I was just about to say.

'Where?' I said.

Neither of us spoke for a little while. We had closed the door of the hut but had not lit the candle. A few dusty rays of sunlight came in through the cracks round the window. The semi-darkness matched our mood.

Warby said, 'What about the tunnel?'

He meant the long one down the embankment.

'The rail's electrified,' I said.

'That's what makes it safe,' said Warby.

'Maybe for the money but what about for us?'

Warby shrugged. 'Got any better ideas?'

I hadn't.

Warby said, 'My brother worked on the railway, he said you just don't touch the insulated track.'

'Which one's that?'

'The ones with porcelain underneath. I'll show you.'

Warby went outside I followed. He pointed out the tracks, and those with porcelain insulators underneath them.

'Suppose you accidentally fall on them?'

'Then you accidentally get burnt up,' said Warby with a laugh, and began to head down the slope. I came carefully after.

Warby was standing on the shingle by the track. He beckoned me to follow. I didn't like it at all. Trains were bad enough but electricity too? Warby was walking along the rails towards the tunnel. He entered the tunnel and I hurried after. I didn't want to be seen down here.

The tunnel was terrifying, the walls black with soot. You could see a little way in and then everything died away in complete darkness. Warby was already some way in. I followed slowly.

It was the dark that frightened me most. Neither could I understand why we were doing it. We hadn't brought the money. In fact we had left it behind for anybody.

I could hardly see Warby now, just a faint shadow along the edge. So small up there.

I shouted, 'Warby.' It echoed in the tunnel.

'Shor-tee,' he called back and it rang around the tunnel. 'Shor-tee,' he called again and again. 'Come on, Shor-tee.'

I'd had enough and stopped when I heard the distant clatter. Warby was running towards me and I could see why. There was a small light growing out of the darkness.

I turned and fled. I was maybe fifty yards in the tunnel, and raced along with wings of fear. I was almost out when my foot caught a sleeper. I stumbled and lost my footing, falling flat out between the rails. I could feel the vibration of the oncoming train, but it was my left hand that terrified me. It was almost touching a rail raised by porcelain insulators.

As I rose I looked back into the noise and the oncoming yellow light. I could just make out the driver of the train, rigid like a man in a model. I couldn't see Warby.

I ran out of the tunnel, and clambered up the bank as if it were a dragon behind me, and hid down behind a shrub just as the train rushed out.

The carriages flashed past. Where was Warby? How much room was there between the tunnel and the edge? I could see a man reading a newspaper, a woman knitting, a girl looking out of the window. And not one of them knew anything about Warby.

The train passed, and I stayed where I was. I could see my hand again as I lay on the track, fingers within inches of the live rail. What would've happened if I'd touched it. Would I have been burnt or been shocked? And if I had been shocked could I have got away from the train?

Warby came out the tunnel. His face, body and hands covered in soot from where he must have pressed himself into the wall. I could see by his shifty look that he'd been very scared. We went back to the signal box and neither of us needed to say that the tunnel was out.

We sat in silence. I lit the candle and Warby stripped to the waist. He was attempting to wipe the soot off his face and hands with his vest. By candlelight it was difficult to see how well he was doing.

He said, 'Your place.'

'Mine? What's wrong with yours?'

He shook his head and began to put on his shirt without the vest. 'I share my room with my brother.'

'Suppose my mum finds it?'

'Does she go in your room?'

'Not very much.'

'Then it has to be your place.'

I didn't like it. It seemed to put everything on me but then I couldn't think of anything better.

'What times does your mum come home from work?'

'About two.'

'We'd better go then.'

Warby was now dressed. He swung a bag over his shoulder. I hesitated.

'Walk through the streets like this?'

Warby laughed. 'Pretend we're going to the launderette.'

9

We left the hut with a sack each. It was only then in the light I could see how unsuccessful Warby had been at cleaning himself up.

'You're filthy.'

He looked at his hands, his clothes and grimaced. 'What's my face like?'

'It's all streaky.' Like a dirty window that the rain had run down.

He shrugged. 'You're not so clean yourself.' It was my turn to look at my hands and clothes. I had obviously touched the sooty walls of the tunnel and my hands had since been leaving the marks on every bit of myself.

'There's nothing we can do,' said Warby. 'Let's just get to your place quickly.'

I climbed over the wall. Warby tossed over the bags and followed after. We crossed over the footbridge and onto the main road. I tried to imagine I was carrying a sack of laundry.

It wasn't that easy to imagine. It was the wrong time of day to begin with. I should be at school now not going to the launderette. I was in the wrong place. The nearest launderette to our flats was in the opposite direction, on the far side of the estate. And I was filthy. You wouldn't send off someone as dirty as I was to wash clothes.

It was hot, the sky cloudless, and the light dazzling after the inside of the signal box. A smell of gravy from the pet food factory sat on us like a mist, making it seem as if we were bits in a stew, about to be prodded and the street wiped up with a lump of bread.

'Everyone's looking at us,' I said.

'You just think they are because you're looking at them.'

I knew that wasn't true but arguing wouldn't have got us there quicker or stopped people looking. Even so I was getting tired of Warby, he always pretended he knew everything and I always seemed to end up going along with his crazy ideas. Like taking these sacks home.

We turned the corner and we saw – and were seen – by a group of girls sitting on the low wall outside the new estate. Amongst them was my sister.

They had their school jackets off and were lounging on the wall eating chips.

Kathy immediately got up and called out. 'What we got 'ere then?' She was smirking as she headed towards us. 'Wanna chip?'

Warby held out his hand and she snatched the bag away.

'You're filthy,' she said.

'Takes one to know one,' said Warby.

Another girl had come up, my sister's best friend,

Sue. She has thin red hair which she ties at the back but it always seems to be trying to escape; like the pleats had all but escaped from her skirt.

'Doing your washing?' she said.

I said, 'We would if people didn't keep stopping us.'

Sue put on a smile showing the braces that kept her teeth from flying off. 'Perhaps we could help.' She gave a low mock bow, clutching her stomach and swinging her other arm almost down to her toes. 'Can I assist you with your bag, sir?'

At which she grabbed the bag I was holding. I fought to pull it away. We tugged and pulled spinning round the pavement. Then Kathy joined in. I held on like a man drowning. Kathy was trying to lever up my fingers. Where was Warby? Sue was drawing the bag away. My sister had prized up my little finger and was bending it back.

'Leggo, you squirt,' yelled Sue as she slowly pushed my hands off the end. The less I had of sack the harder I clasped. I kicked out at my sister. She jumped back and let go of my finger. Sue grabbed my ear and began to twist it.

A scream of surprise from the other girls stopped everything. They were in a huddle, gesticulating and shouting.

'Come here, come here!' one of the girls shouted. Sue and Kathy rushed over.

'Run,' yelled Warby.

I hurtled after Warby. Turning when I was some way off I could see the girls still in a huddle and still excited. They had lost interest in us.

40

We began to walk. For a little while I kept looking behind but they had definitely given up.

'What happened?' I asked.

Warby chuckled. 'They nearly had your sack didn't they?'

'What did you do?'

Smirking he said, 'What do you think?'

In exasperation I said, 'I dunno.'

'I gave them 60 quid.'

His reply shouldn't have surprised me but it did. How else could he have distracted them? It was as if I had forgotten it was money. I had dreamed about the things it could buy. I had dreamed about being caught with it – but I had forgotten it was cash and you could spend it.

I said, 'How did you get it out so quick?'

He looked sheepish. 'I thought something like this might happen so I had it in my pocket.'

I stopped walking. 'How much did you have in your pocket?'

He blew out his cheeks and sniffed. 'A thousand.'

I put down my sack. My blood was boiling. I said, 'If I lie and do you wrong, May the devil slit my tongue.'

Warby hopped from foot to foot. With his free hand he was wiping his ear. 'I didn't lie.'

'We said if any money was to be spent we both had to agree.'

He kicked the brown wooden fence. 'I don't remember that.'

'Anything else you don't remember?'

He turned, his face sour. 'Why did it have to be you?

Why couldn't it have been someone else I found the money with?'

I was punctured. The words waiting to be said died. Warby picked up his sack and without looking at me went walking on. I stuck by the fence and felt utterly miserable. Abandoned by all. Not only was I a lousy criminal, I was friendless too.

I closed my eyes and the darkness swam. I imagined I was hit by a lorry and I was lying there in the road, spread out and dead. Around me was a crowd and Warby with his sack remembering his last words. I felt a hand on my shoulder.

It was a lady in a blue headscarf with a trolley on wheels. She was holding my grey sack. She smiled when I looked up.

'You'll lose this.'

I thanked her.

'You alright?' A tip of dyed black hair with grey roots stuck out of her headscarf.

'I gotta toothache.'

'Get your mum to buy some cloves.'

The second time I had heard that word today. I smiled at her. 'They go in apple pie.'

She laughed. 'You must be older than you look.' Shaking her head and chuckling she rolled on.

I picked up the sack and continued home.

When I got to the flats I saw Warby sitting on a wall. When I got to him he got up and joined me. We didn't talk. We didn't look at each other. I turned into the stairway. I could hear his footsteps behind me. Up the three flights, his footsteps mimicking mine. Along the landing. One door, two door three – and then the blue one. Ours.

I looked in through the letterbox and listened. It wouldn't do to walk in on Mum if she were home early. I couldn't hear anything so I put down the sack.

I searched my pockets for the key. It was after I'd searched my trouser pockets that I began to worry. I never put it in my jacket. I searched my jacket. I began again on my trousers.

I knelt down and began emptying my pockets. A handkerchief, a broken pencil, a bit of string, a couple of nails, a table tennis ball, two picture cards of star constellations, a plastic magnifying glass, several bits of paper but no key. I turned the pockets inside out.

I looked up and met Warby looking down.

He looked as sad as I felt.

'You must've lost it on the railway.'

I nodded. When I hit the tracks I must've lost the key.

Warby lounged against the wall blowing air from his cheeks. I slumped. My head lolled onto my thighs, my eyes in the knees. I heard Warby walk away. I didn't care. Nothing would ever go right again.

I heard him returning. His hand rested on my back.

He said, 'They don't empty the dustbins till Wednesday.'

I looked up at him annoyed. 'What?'

He said, 'Dustbin bags. No one looks inside dustbin bags in the dustbin.'

Was he talking English? He picked up a sack of

money – and it hit me what he was saying. The dust chute!

'Leave 'em there till your mum gets back.'

'Great!' I sprung up.

'Put 'em in one sack and tie the end.'

Warby ran to the stairs at one end and me to the other. No one was coming. We came back together and quickly tipped one sack into the other. We tied the end with the string I knew would be useful one day.

Holding the bag between us we ran down the stairs to the base of the rubbish chute. The door was open. We tossed the sack into the large metal container and left. Free at last!

Warby said, 'Let's spend some money.' He took out a wad of notes.

I said, 'Give me a hundred.'

He counted them out and handed them over. 'What for?'

'For my mum.' And I ran back up the stairs.

10

'Come on,' said Warby, 'let's decide.'

We'd been walking up and down the main shopping centre at East Ham for half an hour. Walking around the stores, looking in the shop windows. We had decided that we didn't want to be seen spending lots of money close to where we lived so we had taken a bus to where we'd be totally unknown.

We'd had a wash in a goldfish pond in a park. Sort of a wash anyway. The loose stuff came off. The other stuff got smudged about. We wiped ourselves on the insides of our shirts. I wouldn't say we were clean. We just weren't so dirty.

I like looking in shop windows. For me a lot of the fun is seeing all the different stuff and imagining having it. Warby wanted to get on with it. And always when it came down to it I didn't. I found a reason for not buying this or that. It was too big, too small, wrong colour. Where would we keep it? I'd seen a better one up West.

The fact was I didn't want to begin. So far although we'd got rid of a bit of money we hadn't spent any ourselves. That's when crime started. When we bought the first thing we'd become criminals. I never worked it out as clear as that – but that's what stopped me buying.

So I just kept finding reasons for not spending anything. Finally that was as obvious to Warby as it was to me.

He walked into a photographic shop. I followed.

A plump young man in a grey suit came up to us. He had a thin moustache like it was drawn with a pencil and talked without hardly moving his lips.

'Can I help you?'

'I'd like that camera,' said Warby.

'This one?' He brought it down from the shelf behind and held it out with a sort of sneer. Like he'd already figured we were mucking him about. Maybe that's what made Warby do it.

'I'll take it,' said Warby.

'That'll be £258,' said the man. I groaned and looked away. Trust Warby to pick one of the most expensive cameras in the shop.

'Right,' said Warby. I turned and watched in horror. He had taken out a bunch of bank notes and was counting them. I watched the young man watching him. Warby had the notes on the counter, '60, 80, 100 . . . '

The plump man's expression hadn't changed but I saw him moving his arm slowly sideways below the counter. Then about a foot away from the rest of his body, it moved a little this way and that. Then stopped and his body stiffened. A few seconds later out of the corner of my eye I saw another grey-suited man across the shop rush to a phone.

Warby was still counting, '180, 200, 220 . . .'

I covered his hand in mine. 'That's not the one you want, Warby.'

Warby was annoyed. 'Leave me alone.'

I grabbed the money and began to leave the shop. Warby followed.

'What's the big idea?'

'The police,' I whispered, 'they're phoning.'

We had got to the door. The young plump man was standing in front of it. Now smiling pleasantly.

'Would you like me to demonstrate it for you, sir. Perhaps you'd like a go yourself. Single lens reflex, automatic and manual, through the lens metering, bayonet fitting . . .'

He moved as we moved. I turned. The other greysuited man was coming in on us.

Warby went one way, I went the other. The plump man tried to go both ways at once and dropped the camera. We got out the door.

And ran. We seemed to be spending a lot of time running. We cut off the main road and down a side street. Down along, cutting through, putting distance and confusion between us and the camera shop. We came to a park, followed the fence until we arrived at the entrance, found a patch of grass and collapsed.

After a few minutes I sat up.

'That was pretty daft.'

Warby rolled over onto his front. In a sulky voice he said, 'Go boil your head.'

'You shoulda seen yourself. A wad of notes like a millionaire.'

Warby rolled onto his back and sat up. 'What's the point of all that money if we can't spend it?'

'No point.'

'So we've either got to be able to spend it or get rid of it.'

Yes that was it. We had oodles of it and Warby had put it plain. I laid on my back and looked into the trees, like a half-completed jigsaw against the sky. I didn't want to spend my life running with a sack.

'Suppose we put it in the bank,' said Warby.

'How much at a time?'

Warby looked a little nervous. 'Say £40 a day.'

'Why not say fifty, say a hundred, say a thousand. Say anything you like.'

'You can be a pain.'

'I stopped you getting arrested.'

Warby sighed heavily. 'Yeh.' He stretched out and slapped my hand. 'Thanks.'

'At £40 a day . . . ' I had taken out a piece of paper and was working on a sum. 'It would take 25 days to bank £1000. So 246 times 25 divided by 365 . . . Jesus.'

'I don't think we can open a bank account on our own anyway,' said Warby miserably.

'We could get a post office book,' I said, still working on the sum.

'Suppose . . . ' Warby's hand had gone to his mouth, he was getting excited, 'we got a post office book each. Or maybe we could have six each. Using different names at different offices. Yes twelve books!' He turned to me. 'Work that out, Shorty.'

'Hang on,' I said. 'OK – with one book, putting £40 a day, that'd take seventeen years.'

'Can't be right.' He was looking over my shoulders, I could hear him fighting with the figures as he checked mine.

'So with twelve books,' I continued, 'putting the same away in each would take about . . . one and a half years.'

Warby was scratching his ear and biting his fist at the same time. 'How many books would you need to put it all away in four weeks.'

'Warby!'

'Go on,' he said urgently, 'work it out.'

I scribbled on. 'First thing we should've got is not a camera but a calculator . . . '

'In just a month,' he said excitedly, 'we could go running around and then it'd all be safe and we could get it whenever we wanted at any time we wanted.'

'You can only get £100 a time out of the post office.'

'That's with one book.'

I carried on with the sum. 'Putting away £40 a day in each book for a month you would need . . . 204 books.' I burst out laughing uncontrollably. 'Where we going to find 204 post offices, 204 names, 204 different addresses . . . '

'It could be done,' said Warby angrily. 'It'd just take some travelling about.'

'Some travelling about! Going to 204 post offices every day . . . '

'There's two of us.'

I shrugged. 'Think how far the furtherest one'd be. Maybe Southend. Going there everyday.'

'I like Southend.'

'And getting off at every stop on the way, every day. You know how much money we'd each be carrying around with us? £4080! And putting it away £40 at a time. You're crackers, Warby.'

'It could be done.'

'You couldn't even buy a camera.'

That'd stung and I knew it. Warby got up and started walking. I lay back looking into the trees. How many leaves on it? Two hundred and forty-six thousand?

Where would we put 204 post office books? If each one was an eighth of an inch thick . . . I couldn't stop doing sums! That'd make twenty-five inches. More than two foot of post office books!

A thought made me laugh. It makes me laugh now even as I write it down. I got a post office book and every so often they take the book off you and send it to head office and then post it back to you. So Warby's amazing idea couldn't work. They'd send them back to all our 204 phony addresses! That was so funny. All these books going everywhere. All sorts of people getting post office books in the mail in the name of someone they'd never heard of. All the money split up into 204 different places!

Warby was standing over me. He was smiling. He said, 'Forget post office books.'

'Forgotten,' I said, but still laughing at my thought.

He said, 'I couldn't spend £258 on a camera. Why's that?'

'You're justa kid, that's why.'

'Right,' said Warby. 'We need an adult.'

11

That's Warby for you. Sometimes so stupid he should be locked up for his own safety. Like the money in the camera shop or Warby in the tunnel. And other times he's there. Right on top of it before anybody.

Too quick for me. I was nearly at the point where I'd done with the money. Then Warby jumps in and we're off.

'An adult?' I said.

'An adult,' said Warby.

I kept saying the word and thinking of the adults I knew. My mum – tell her? – no thanks. Teachers – might as well tell the police. My dad – I'd get walloped round the borough.

'I don't know anyone,' I said.

Warby said, 'Yes you do.'

'I do?'

Warby was nodding his head in a knowing way. 'Think of the sort of person it's got to be.'

'What d'you mean?'

Warby sighed heavily. 'Would your mum do it?'

'Course not.'

'Well why?'

'She's too honest.'

'Right. So what sort of person do we want?'

'Someone bent.'

'And what else?'

'Someone we get along with. Someone who can keep their mouth shut. Someone who won't cause us any trouble. Someone who's got a job, who looks like they've got money.' I was getting the hang of it but something was missing. Then it came. 'Someone who needs money.'

'How about someone who gambles?'

'Eddie,' I shouted.

Eddie's got a stall in the market. He's a ted, but pretty old – I should say about forty. He gives us a bit if we do a stint on the stall so he can put a bet on.

'We'll have to tell him carefully,' I said.

'No trouble,' said Warby rubbing his hands. 'We offer him a job. He's in our employ. We just tell him as much as we need to.'

The day had come over cloudy. A chilly wind was blowing through the trees. We decided to walk home.

When we got to the flats the estate looked gloomier than ever. There was never any colour to it. Some houses, some streets have a welcome to them. They look interesting. You know people like living there. You look in the windows and you know it's their home. Like they look like they belong in it, it's cosy. In our flats I always feel like a mouse that's been chased into its hole.

Warby said, 'We got to get the money in.'

'Can't do it now. My mum'll be in.'

'What time she go to bed?'

'About eleven.'

'I'll meet you at the chute at twelve.'

We parted and I went upstairs. I was thinking about Eddie. We'd arranged to see him tomorrow, late afternoon when the market was clearing up. The more I thought about Eddie the less sure I got. Eddie was too much like Warby.

At the front door I started searching for my key. Then I remembered I lost it. I rapped the knocker.

Kathy answered. She put a finger to her lips, glanced behind her and said in a whisper,

'He's here.'

'Who?'

'Dad.'

The kitchen was full of smoke. Mum was sitting at the table shelling peas, a cigarette beside her in an ashtray. Her face looked as if it were about to melt.

Dad was sitting at the table, drinking tea and smoking. He was very clean.

'Hello, Davey.'

'Hello, Dad.'

Mum began to cry. She covered her face with her hands and her body jerked with sobs.

Dad said, 'What a welcome.'

Kathy said stiffly, 'What'd you expect?'

'Maybe not the welcome mat but this is my family.'

Kathy said, 'Look what you do to her.'

The kitchen was crowded out. The four of us, Mum and Dad sitting at the table. Me leaning against the sink, Kathy against the kitchen cabinet. Mum sobbing quietly now, wiping her face with her hand, Dad trying to look unconcerned, leaning back in the chair, drawing on the cigarette, looking like he owned the place.

'So how's tricks, Davey?'

'Alright.'

'You getting on at school?'

'Yeh.'

'He's top in maths,' said Kathy.

'That's good. Very good. Whatever you do you need maths.'

I wanted him to go. I could see Mum couldn't handle it and I'd certainly got used to him not being around this last year. Life had been quieter, steadier. I'd been able to sleep at night.

But he didn't look like he was about to go.

'And you're becoming a young lady, Kath.'

'No thanks to you.' She screwed her face and didn't look at him.

'Now was that called for?' he said in a most reasonable voice, as if there were a jury in the room who could say it wasn't.

He was wearing a light zip jacket and under it a white T-shirt. He definitely looked well, although his hair was thinning at the front. My hair. He was short too, same eyes as me. Better looking than me though. Difficult to say why, his face was too thin and bony – but it was alive. It could light up and shine everything in its light. If you didn't know him.

'You staying?' asked Kathy, putting the question we were all thinking.

Dad said, 'I don't seem very welcome.' I think he

wanted one of us to say he was. No one answered. Mum had gone back to shelling the peas. The peas popping in the pan seemed very loud.

'So you staying?' said Kathy.

He turned his head and looked at her. 'Do you want me to?'

Kathy sniffed and turned her head away. 'It's not up to me.'

A tough smile had come to his face. 'I didn't ask whether it was up to you.'

'When you're here it's trouble,' she said.

Dad turned to me. 'Two women ganging up against me. What's me lad think?'

I shrugged.

'That's not much of an answer.'

I shrugged again.

'How'd you find us?' said Kathy.

'It wasn't easy.'

Suddenly Mum sighed. Her eyes were closed, she clenched the pan.

'For God sake, George – why torture us?'

Dad had gone white. I could hear him slowly breathing. I could hear the whole room breathing.

'Why don't you go?' said Kathy.

He turned to her. 'Some daughter you are.'

'Some dad,' she said quietly.

He rose and started towards her. Then stopped. He looked around the room at each one of us in turn.

'I was looking forward to this.'

He plunged a hand in his pocket and drew out a box of chocolates. He threw it on the table. I caught his eye for an instant, there were tears in the corners. I looked away. Mum was still clutching the pot between both hands, eyes shut.

Then he was gone from the room.

12

I lay on the bed. I was hungry and supper was late. I felt rotten. Mum was crying in the other room and I was crying too, but without tears.

It was the cold miseries. Lying over me like a sheet. The world's rotten, I'm rotten and that is the way it is going to stay. Rotten. Why be alive when you could be dead.

I knew it was all connected with Dad's visit. Everything's going alright and there he is. And I know wherever he is, is the worse for me. And I wasn't thinking of Mum or Kathy. Wherever he is, is the worse for me.

I wanted to cry my heart out. Cry out all that misery and loneliness. But my eyes were dry. Like I was too unhappy to cry.

Kathy came in. I clenched my eyes tight and let out a sigh. I wanted her to know I was suffering.

'It was you – wasn't it?'

'What?' I said into the blanket.

'The hundred quid.'

I had forgotten that. The money I had left a century ago, at dinner-time.

'No.'

'She thinks it was him and she won't spend it. I don't think it was him.'

I turned over. She was standing above me like a totem pole. Her face had a determined look, cruel perhaps or maybe that was just the way I felt. Relatives used to say she was pretty but I never saw it. Or maybe prettiness is something you only see from a distance. Me and my sister we had fought and argued, we had been miserable together. We looked too close; there wasn't room to stand back and see each other like others did.

'Only me and you knew she owed 98 quid. So who gives her a hundred, who with a best friend who gave out 60 as if it were last week's Radio Times?'

'What you on about?'

'You know Warby gave us 60 quid – didn't you?'

'No.'

Her eyebrows raised in arch surprise. 'Oh you didn't know did you? We all know and he doesn't tell his best friend?' Her lip curled. 'If you are going to tell lies you'd better do better than that.'

Yes I had.

'I meant I knew but I didn't know where he got it.'

'And you're nothing to do with it?'

'Nothing.'

'Liar.'

I turned over into the bedclothes. 'Why don't you ever believe me?'

'Because my brother tells lies.'

And my sister is too clever. It's always been that

59

way. She always knows when I'm up to something. No matter what I say.

'Will you leave me alone?'

'Why should I?'

Into the dark of the blanket. 'I feel rotten that's why.'

'Dinner's ready.'

'I'm not hungry.'

'Don't make things worse for Mum.' And I heard her leave.

When I slouched into the kitchen Kathy and Mum were sitting at the table. The plate of food waiting for me turned my stomach over.

'You know I don't like potato salad.'

Mum said, 'I can't keep up with what you like and dislike.'

'I've never liked it.'

'Well you'll just have to eat it.'

I sat down and pushed the potato salad to one side of the plate, and then shovelled the hated mayonnaise along with it. It had been sitting on the lettuce, and had flowed into the peas – both were ruined for me. The tomato and the tuna looked alright. I took a forkful of the tuna – as it came close I smelt it.

'You know I don't like vinegar on tuna.'

Mum said, 'Do you like anything?'

I eat the couple of slices of tomato.

'You're as bad as your father,' she said.

I wished I'd stayed in my room.

'What's the point making anything if you don't eat it?'

It was pointless saying anything. I stretched out for the bread.

'Leave that,' she said, and took the bread away. 'I will not have you waste all that food.'

'I don't like it,' I said.

She slapped me round the face. My head rang with the pain of it. Tears came and I forced them back.

'Now eat it.'

I stuck a fork in a piece of potato salad and brought it to my mouth. My stomach responded to the taste by threatening to throw up. I chewed slowly, poisoning my tongue and my throat. I held down my guts as I swallowed.

When I looked up Mum was crying.

'Leave it,' she said, 'leave it.'

I put down my fork.

'Go on – have some bread,' she said through her tears.

I didn't want bread now but I took a slice and buttered it. It took away the taste of the mayonnaise.

'I'll make some tea,' said Kathy, and got up to put on the kettle.

Mum dabbed her eyes with a tissue. Her cheeks were red and puffy; new tears on top of old.

'He'll be back,' she said. Neither of us needed to ask who.

I slapped the bread around my mouth. Everything she said seemed to be heard through the burn of my cheek.

'When the pub shuts,' she added.

I wished I was an orphan. No dad to come back with dirty promises, no mum to slap me.

'Can I go now?' I said.

'Is that all you are going to eat?'

I nodded.

'Have an apple.' I took one. 'I'm sorry,' she said and took my hand. She held it to her face. 'You're getting such a big boy now.' She shook her head. 'You need a father.'

'I don't need him.'

She sighed. 'I can't give you the time. Both of you – I'm not being fair.' She looked into my eyes. They were still wet. 'I didn't mean it.'

'You didn't have to hit me.'

She started blubbing. 'You should never hit anybody. Nobody should ever hit anybody.'

Kathy came over and put her arm round her. She leaned against Kathy sniffing. She let go of my hand.

I wanted someone to lean on.

I watched my sister and my mother. They were beyond my reach. It's always been that way. Kathy was Dad's favourite too.

I went back to my room.

13

Can you die of unhappiness? I expect you can't except in fairy stories – but it feels like you can. Like you got a hole in you that's growing and growing. Until one day you're empty as a bubble. And pop! There's nothing.

It's difficult looking back and trying to think what I was thinking then. When Dad had gone and Mum and Kathy were together in the kitchen. Not so much as difficult as – well I don't want to say it. Like I said in the beginning how much do I tell you about me. It would be a whole lot easier if I just stuck to the action.

What makes it difficult – I think I got it now – is it's so stupid. Kids' stuff. I was nearly thirteen. Did other people think like me?

Half the time I wanted to be dead. But not really dead because I wanted to see them seeing me. Like going to my own funeral to see who came and who would be sorry. I dreamed that. Mum there, Kathy there, Dad there – standing around a hole where I was. All looking miserable. And me standing with 'em to make sure they're miserable enough.

But I had the money. And why be dead with all that money? I'd make 'em sorry. When I had so much and they wanted some of it. When they tried to be nice to me then I'd remind 'em of now.

Kathy would come to the house and the butler would announce her – and I would say I am not in. I would watch her slouching back down the gravel drive to the gate, old and tearful. And I would say to myself – fine to cry now, but what about then? How horrid you were then, and you won't get a dud penny now.

That's how I was thinking. Or trying to think because I couldn't hold it all together. Each dream killed the other. Dead was dead. You couldn't be nearly dead. Nearly dead wasn't dead enough. And if I were rich? Suppose my mother wouldn't take anything? I thought of the £100 she wouldn't spend. Suppose she said, 'No. I love Kathy. I don't want your money. You keep your big house, David. Me and Kathy will manage somehow.'

That wasn't the point of it at all.

I built a rocket ship and filled it with food, videos and books, and space equipment. And I put an advert in the paper for two companions to explore Space. And never come back.

I waited for them to come and say don't go. Please don't go away forever. My mum came and that's what she did say. She cried and said she loved me and how she would miss me. I said I have to go.

We travelled in overdrive, watching as earth got tinier and tinier. And all those who had made us suffer got tinier with it. We drunk champagne when earth disappeared.

My dreams are stupid. Some cruel, like I wouldn't

want to tell you some of 'em. In a way I can understand someone like Hitler. In my dreams I could easily put the world in a sack and drown it in the canal. I get that mood when I could kill everybody and anything.

Anyway I was feeling all like that in a sort of half awake half sleep when a tap on the window broke it. I thought 'Dad!' The pubs were shut and he was back. Not him.

I bit my knuckle, sinking my teeth deep between the bones. Go away.

'Shorty,' a whispered voice called.

With relief I realized it was Warby. I got up and went to the window.

My bedroom is a front room. It opens onto the walkway. For a second I could see nothing. Then a few stars sprinkled around the shadow of the next block. A torch light shone and there was Warby crouching under the window.

'I bin waiting ages.'

I'd forgotten I was supposed to meet him at the chute.

'Let's do it tomorrow.'

'I done it already.'

He lifted up a smelly bag.

14

'Mailman bring me no more bloo-oos,

   'One bloo letter is all I can use.'

Eddie was singing the same lines over and over as he packed up the stall. All around us stallholders were taking down poles, and putting their goods away. Between the stalls were heaps of litter; cardboard boxes, squashed fruit, straw. We edged around Eddie trying to catch his eye.

Eddie continued singing and carrying boxes to his van as if we weren't there.

'We got some business,' said Warby.

Eddie stopped. 'Look kiddo. I gotta get home, have a bath, wash me hair and be out to the Grapes by seven-thirty. Any other night I'd be glad to discuss business. But not . . . ' He started to sing. 'Saturday night at the movies, who cares what the picture may be-ee.'

He gave Warby a pat on the face, grinned at him and picked up a box. His large tattooed arms swung it in tune onto the van.

Eddie's a ted. I think he's always been one since they first came in. He goes to the Grapes where they play fifties music. Sometimes he does a spot as DJ. Late Saturday afternoon he was getting into the mood. We were just in his way.

We hung around thinking how to interrupt him. Eddie was already at the Grapes. His feet were skipping to his own tune. When he put a box down, he clicked his fingers, twisted his body and threw back his head as if he were on stage and did a couple of slick steps before picking up another box.

I nudged Warby. 'Let's see him Monday.'

Warby gave me a sour look. 'Why d'you want to do everything tomorrow?'

I shrugged. 'Why you always in such a rush?'

He punched a hand into his fist. 'If you want to do something – do it now!'

Eddie was busy in the back of the van. Warby strode up to the stall, shoved some bank notes on a box and quickly backed off. We watched Eddie.

He came from the van singing and made out he was looking in a mirror, saying what a great guy I am. He slicked forward his greased overhanging hair and brushed down his sideburns that ran down his craggy face almost to his chin.

He saw the money and stopped his playing. 'What's this?'

'First instalment,' said Warby.

He picked up the money and looked it carefully over. Sniffed it, flicked it. 'For what?'

Warby swaggered up to him. 'How'd you like to work for us?'

Eddie let out a sudden roar of laughter, and thumped Warby on the back. Warby looked offended.

'I thought you meant it, kiddo.' He picked up a box.

Warby stood his ground. 'What would you say to 400 a week?'

I grabbed Warby's sleeve. He pushed me away.

'Starting now.' Warby was holding a fistful of notes. Eddie dropped his box and came across.

'Where'd you get all this?' he said in a hushed voice. Warby put it away and turned his back.

'You wanna talk business, Eddie.'

Eddie licked his lower lip. 'Yeh.' He looked about him. 'Not here.' He indicated us with a crooked finger to come in closer. 'Meet me in the rec in half an hour.'

We kicked a cardboard box around the market. Warby was pleased with himself and I was impressed. He'd done it like a natural, as if he did deals like this everyday. That last bit when he turned his back – it said, 'take it or leave it, Eddie.'

'See how I did it, Shorty.'

'Like a pro.'

'A few days and we'll be drinking out of gold cups.'

Warby said it'd be good technique to let Eddie get to the rec first. As if we were doing him a favour bringing him in. We kicked around and ran about until we were about ten minutes late and then went over to the rec.

Eddie was pacing around by the drinking fountain. When he saw us he indicated a spot on the grass.

We sat down. Eddie gave us a broad smile.

'Gum?' He offered us a stick each.

68

Warby refused. I took my cue from him. We weren't going to be bought with a stick of gum.

'So,' said Eddie, 'you come into a bit of money.'

'A bit,' said Warby.

'How much?'

'Enough.'

'Enough for what?'

'Enough to keep a sea lion in fish.'

Eddie grinned at me. 'Smart your mate, eh?'

'He knows what's what,' I said.

Eddie sucked his lip. 'So what'dje need me for?'

'Thought you might like to work for us,' said Warby.

'Work!' He spat the word out. 'Me work for a couple of kids with some hot money?' His grin had changed. It wasn't good-humoured anymore. He was laughing at us.

'You two get picked up flashing fistfuls and I get five years. No thanks!'

'So you're not interested eh?' said Warby and started to get up.

'Hang about,' said Eddie in a sweeter tone.

Warby said, 'You don't want to work for a couple of kids you said.' I had got up too.

Eddie said, 'I bin inside once and I ain't too keen to repeat it.'

'I understand,' said Warby. 'Sorry we wasted your time.' We began to walk off.

Eddie called, 'If you want some financial management, come here and sit down.'

Warby turned. 'There's more than you can give it, Eddie.'

'Got a big list have you?' said Eddie laughing. 'All keen to do five years eh?'

It was then I realized that Warby had started walking off too quick. He'd got himself into a spot where all he could do was keep walking or come back. Like he'd pulled away too quick and I could see Eddie knew that Warby didn't mean it. Warby wanted to be called back and if no one did it would just show how much he needed Eddie.

'Let's hear what he's got to say,' I said to Warby.

Warby stayed his ground. 'He don't want to listen to kids.' He was stuck on the spot. He couldn't come or go unless Eddie asked him to.

'Come on,' I said, playing the soft man. 'No harm listening.'

Warby was stuck. And I was piggy in the middle trying to draw them together.

'Your mate's right,' said Eddie to Warby, reckoning it was time to draw in his fish. 'I got a few things to say you might find interesting.'

'I guess there's no harm in listening.' And Warby returned to the circle. You could see he was relieved.

'Now,' said Eddie, 'tell me when I go wrong. You got some money – and it's hot. I won't ask how you got it. Now you got a problem or you wouldn't need me. Right so far?'

'Carry on,' I said.

'Your problem could be that the law is on to you. If so then count me out.'

'That's not the problem,' I said.

'Then that just leaves the money itself. How to

70

dispose of it. How to do what you want with it. Made more difficult because you are a pair of juveniles. Yes?' He gave us the broadest of smiles.

Warby looked unhappy. Eddie had sized us up, and that left little room for his playing the big man.

'Yes,' I said.

Warby was playing with his fingernails.

'So,' he went on, 'you need someone to launder the money.'

'Launder?' I asked.

'Make it safe. Change it from hot money to regular money. So when a cop says where did you get that thousand you don't have to say I robbed a bank but I sold a car and here's the receipt, or I won it on a horse and the betting office will bear me out? Get me?'

We nodded.

'Now small amounts I can launder on the stall. Say I got from a day's sales. But I can't do that with thousands. You got thousands or what?'

'Thousands,' I said.

Warby was sulking. He'd got out of his depth and didn't like it that I was doing the talking.

'How many thousands?'

I looked to Warby. Warby looked back at me a warning in his eye.

'I need to know,' said Eddie. 'If it's going to be laundered I need to know what I'm dealing with.'

Neither of us answered.

At last I said, 'You're asking lots of questions and we don't know whether you're in or out yet.'

71

Eddie scratched his sideburn, then said, 'I'll work for you, but only if you do exactly what I say.'

Warby looked up. 'We keep the money.'

'OK,' said Eddie, 'but when it comes to spending it you do what I say.'

We looked to each other. I didn't feel comfortable and I guessed Warby felt the same. I said, 'We gotta talk this over.'

'Sure,' said Eddie.

Me and Warby walked off a bit.

'What do you think?' I said.

Warby walked a circle shaking his head. 'We gotta watch him.'

'Long as he don't know how much or where it is.'

Warby suddenly gave me a sharp look. 'I don't even know where it is.'

I was offended. 'It's under my bed.'

'Flipping hell. What happens when your mum gives a sweep?'

'She don't do it often.'

'And if she does it tomorrow?'

I couldn't answer. I mean she might.

He indicated Eddie lying on the grass singing 'Jailhouse Rock'. 'Let's sign him up.'

We went back and told him it was on.

'Shake,' said Eddie. We did a three-handed shake. 'I want to think it out over the weekend. Maybe sound out a few contacts. 'Don't worry, I won't tell them nothing. In the meantime I want 200 for myself to seal our bargain so to speak. And as for you two . . . '

Eddie got out a bundle of notes from his inside pockets. He counted some off.

'I don't want you spending that big money. Here's 20 in ones. If anyone asks – you did an afternoon on the stall for me.'

15

We finally had some real money.

'What we going to do with it?' I said.

Warby smiled. 'Spend it.'

'I wasn't thinking of burning it. What on?'

'Let's have a hamburger and think about it.'

We crossed the main road and headed up the street to the hamburger bar. It was early and the streets were quiet. People were at home, feet up for a night in front of the box or running the bath for a night out.

The hamburger bar was empty. The cook was talking to the waitress, who was leaning over the counter, standing on one leg. She had a loud cackle of a laugh like she'd just been told a dirty joke. As we came in they both pulled away as if they'd been caught doing something they shouldn't. She brushed herself down and picked up her notebook. He turned to the stove.

We sat by the window. We wanted to see what was out there and be seen by whoever came by. The menu was one of those on a board, with pictures of what's on offer just in case you can't read.

The waitress stood over us. She had a smell of onions and soap you buy your mum at Christmas. I couldn't stop looking at her lips; they were really red like blood and she kept sucking them as she waited for us. Like she ate raw meat when no one was looking.

Warby said, 'I'll have a knickerbocker glory, a mixed grill, and a coke.'

I said, 'I'll have a banana milk shake, a quarter pounder and chips, a fizzy orange and a slice of strawberry cream cake.'

She rested her arms on the table. Here it comes I thought. She had that look teachers give you when you've given a smart answer and they're stuck for a smart reply.

'You got the money for this?'

They were so red, not so much like blood, more like poppies. And shiny that when they creased as she spoke, it was as if they were plastic.

'Yes,' said Warby and put £5 on the table.

Her lips closed like an anemone and she sniffed. 'You'll need more than that.'

Warby pulled out the rest. I wanted to cover my face.

'Won't be a minute,' she said and walked quickly to the counter. She began talking quietly to the cook.

'You shouldn't flash it, Warby.'

'S'only twenty.'

'You needn't have done that though.'

They were talking away and kept looking in our direction. I was beginning to think I've been here before and I started to look at the door for a getaway when she called over, 'Do you want the sundaes first?'

'Yes,' called back Warby.

She began to prepare them and I could see that the

cook had begun work. They had decided to take our money.

Warby was rubbing his hands. 'Am I looking forward to this.'

'This is how the rich live,' I said. 'The cook comes in and gives them a menu. Anything they want, anytime they want. Snap of the fingers and everyone's running after them.'

Warby said, 'I think we should get a car.'

'We can't drive.'

'A chauffeur-driven car.'

I looked at Warby blankly. I tried to imagine a chauffeur-driven car pulling into our flats. People'd think it was a funeral.

'Not a car, Warby.'

'I want a car.' He had put on that I won't be argued-with voice.

'What about your mum and dad?'

'They can have a lift if they want one.' He laughed.

I laughed. 'Imagine,' I giggled, 'stopping at a bus stop and giving Kershaw a lift.'

This rolled us both up.

'His face,' I stammered.

Warby sat up stiffly, his nose in the air and flipped his fingers. 'Kier Hardie School, James, and don't spare the horse.'

'Everyone's waiting for the school bus to go to the pitches and we go by in a Rolls.'

'And get changed in the back,' laughed Warby.

The waitress was coming over with our sundaes. We sat up properly, tried to stop giggling. Warby smirked then broke into a laugh and that dragged me in and we were both rolling up again. By the time we had stopped she had come and gone.

I tried to keep a straight face. Warby smiled and I burst out laughing and Warby joined in.

'Stop it,' I said and looked out the window, straight into the face of Sue and my sister making faces at us through the window.

Sue had her nose pressed against the window and her fingers flat, showing white against the glass. Kathy had her tongue stuck on the pane. When they saw me looking at them they began pulling their mouths and bulging their cheeks. I turned away.

'We've had it now,' I said.

'Just ignore 'em', said Warby. 'Drink your milk shake.'

Ignore my sister? Sooner ignore a charging elephant. I tried concentrating on my milk shake. Milk shakes deserve to be concentrated on, they don't come that often. But it was impossible not to see my sister and Sue.

'Let's move,' said Warby.

We picked up our sundaes and moved into the shop. We sat in a cubicle with our backs to the window.

I hoped they would go away. I prayed for it. But maybe the prayers of the wicked aren't answered. I heard the door swing. It had to be.

It was. They sat down at our table all smiles. Just as they did so our waitress came over and put down our main courses. She stood over us, her anemone slightly open.

'What would you like, girls?'

Kathy said, 'I'll have a pineapple sundae, and a double whopper and chips.'

'Me too,' said Sue. 'And a coke.'

'Oh yes,' said Kathy, 'a coke. A large one. With ice.'

The waitress looked us over. 'Who's paying for all this?'

'Me,' said Warby. 'S'my birthday.'

''Appy returns,' said the waitress and left us.

'Must be nice to be six,' said Sue in a silly voice.

My sister said in mock serious voice, 'You must have a good job, Warby.'

'Civil Service,' said Warby.

'Most Civil I bet,' said Sue.

'Who did you rob?' said Kathy.

Warby smiled, that sweet freckly, innocent smile of his. 'Was that question addressed to me, young lady?'

'Shall I put it in an envelope with your card, birthday boy?' she said in a tone I knew so well.

'Better than a pair of old knickers,' said Warby and got us all laughing.

Sue nudged Kathy. 'He didn't answer your question did he?'

Kathy put a finger to the side of her forehead and twirled it.

'Poor kid,' said Sue shaking her head, 'and so young.'

'His mum dropped him,' said Kathy, 'and some say,' she continued in a loud whisper, 'she did it on purpose.'

It was difficult to eat with Kathy there. All the questions I know she had. The two of 'em watching, making fun while we had our platefuls. I could feel my face burning. Questions. Kathy was too sharp for our answers.

'So no jokes,' she said. 'Where's it all come from?'

Warby said, 'We found it in an old house.'

I choked. Warby hit me on the back.

'While the owners were out for the night?' said Kathy.

'A derelict house,' said Warby.

'Lucky that,' said Sue.

'Very lucky,' said Warby.

'Find much?' said Kathy, continuing the quiz.

'A couple of hundred thou.'

'Wouldn't like to lend me 50,000?' said Kathy. 'Just for tonight. I left me purse at home.'

'My mum said never lend money.'

'Alright give it to me.'

'Whatever you get too easy you don't appreciate.'

While Kathy was asking the questions Sue was looking very hard at Warby, like she was trying to drill into his head. She said, 'Spose I tell your mum, Peter Warburton?'

'And what you done with that 60 I give you?'

Sue looked down at her hands. 'What 60?'

'How much you got?' said Kathy.

'I told you,' said Warby.

'Don't make me laugh.'

The waitress came with their food. She put the bill on the table. Warby picked it up and sorted out his money. He gave her a bundle of notes.

'Keep the change.' He stood up. 'Enjoy your meal.'

I'd only half finished and my cream slice was still due but I was keen to get out. Kathy would just keep pushing and pushing.

Out on the street I said, 'Let's go to the pictures.'

'Love to,' said Warby. 'One thing.'

'What?'

'We're broke.'

16

The market's closed Mondays so we went to his lock-up round the corner. Eddie was loading shirts into his van, singing to the world.

'Peggy Soo, I love you,
'With a love so pure and troo
'O Peggy, my Peggy Soo-oo-oo.'

He grunted on the 'oo-oo-oo' as if he were dying of love. Every bit of his body loved her; you could see it, and a second's separation was going to be lethal.

We stood waiting. He played up for us. Got down on one knee and made out he was holding a micro-phone and as if Warby was the girl. After a final 'oo-oo-oo-oo-oo' his heart broke and he died on the pavement.

We clapped. Eddie got up all smiles. He went to a box of shirts.

'You wanna shirt? Have a shirt?'

They were all the same, a dark green check. Not bad though. Me and Warby took one each.

Eddie rubbed his hands. 'I bin busy, kiddos and I got a scheme for you that's got cream on top.' He looked about him and then said in a dramatic whisper. 'How'd you like to be in on a circus?'

Warby's eyes became like saucers. 'With lions?'

Eddie walked about us, cool. 'With lions, with horses, with elephants, with dogs, with sea lions. They even got a boxing kangaroo. Bareback riders, jugglers, gymnasts, fire eaters, escape artists – you name it.' He took out a creased leaflet from his back pocket and handed it over. It said Beecham's Circus, Yorkshire's own, and had a picture of lions on tubs roaring at a trainer holding a whip.

Warby saw it and went wild. He held an imaginary chair and whip, and was holding off the three big cats. 'Up! Up! Through! Through!'

I wasn't such easy meat.

'How's it work?' I said, holding myself back.

'Well,' says Eddie washing his hands, 'the money you got now ain't yours. You spend a penny of it and everyone knows it ain't yours. Right?'

We nodded.

'It ain't got no legitimacy. You spend 100 quid and the old bill asks you where you got 100 quid you ain't got no answer. But the circus . . . ' He smiled like a sun and patted Warby, who was also shining brightly, 'gives you leg-it-im-ac-y.' He tapped Warby lightly for each syllable.

'It's laundered see. You got part of a circus, right, and have every right to receive income from it.'

One bit was still sticking on me. 'How would we say we got it in the first place?'

Eddie laughed. 'Sharp pair of kids, you're with me all the way. It's a beaut. You'll love it.' He kissed his hand and blew a kiss to the imaginary throng.

'You're going to get left it in a will. Nice eh? You got an uncle in the circus. Not really an uncle but you bin calling him uncle for years and he's going to leave you it in his will.'

'We can't both have an uncle.'

'Why not?' says Eddie. 'There's this old geezer, you bin doing his garden for years. You ain't even told anyone. You didn't know he was rich, or part owner of a circus in Yorkshire. Not even his neighbours know. Miser see? Then Lord Gor Lumme he snuffs it and leaves you the circus in his will.' Eddie flicked his fingers. 'You're legitimate as Elvis.'

''Mazing!' cooed Warby. He'd been sold from the first mention of animals. The rest was all cherries on top. He turned to me. 'We can even tell our mums.'

Eddie said, 'Leave that to me. One day you get a letter inviting you and your parents to a solicitor. It's all explained. We just coach the two of you in the story, make sure you got the names, dates and places right – then it's Bob's your uncle.'

Warby stretched his hands wide. 'Local Kids make Big.'

'That's it – big splash. Then everyone knows. Photos, interviews. Then you're celebrities and you can spend money how you like cuz everyone knows you got it. What do you think?'

'Brilliant,' said Warby.

I was impressed, nervous of the publicity and the story we would have to stick to.

'So when do we get to see this . . . er,' I looked at the leaflet again, 'Beecham's Circus?'

83

'Well,' said Eddie, 'we wanna get this on the move. The thought of you two sitting on quarter of a million . . .'

I jerked. 'How did you know how much?'

Eddie rubbed his nose with a finger. 'How much money you think disappears? Big money? I asked about didn't I? And there's some very disappointed geezers . . .'

I remembered the three men quarrelling outside the house.

'They ain't nice fellars,' said Eddie, 'and the quicker we can get that money out from wherever you have stashed it, to some legitimate set up, the safer we are all going to feel.'

That was sense alright. Those three would shove us down a drainhole and pour sauce on top.

Eddie got his wallet out. 'You meet the owner tomorrow. In Leeds. You catch the eleven o'clock train from King's Cross, change at Doncaster and catch the local. He'll meet you at Leeds station. Take the money.'

'All of it?' I said.

'The lot,' said Eddie. 'We don't want no hot money about.'

'Hang about,' I said. 'We wanna discuss it.'

'Sure.'

I drew Warby to one side.

Warby was still on fire. 'What a chance.'

'I don't like it.'

'Just what do you like, Shorty?' retorted Warby.

'Look – you know what it was like just taking the money home. You fancy going up by train with it?'

'You want it left under your bed? Do you?'

He shot me down.

'Suppose the deal's no good,' I said.

'Then we don't hand over.'

I thought about it. I felt uncomfortable, but I was having too many sleepless nights with that sack underneath me. It had to go and if this worked we had 'legitimacy'.

'Alright.'

Warby switched the sun back on. We returned to Eddie and told him.

'This'll be the making of you, lads.'

He gave us fare in small notes and spending money for the journey.

'No more hand-outs after this, see?'

We left Eddie with his heart breaking again for Peggy Sue. Half the borough must know.

17

It's alright for Warby. Any crazy idea and he's off running – but I wasn't happy. Warby says I worry too much but I don't reckon he worries enough.

Eddie's idea scared me. We had to take another day off. Well that was the least of it. Then we had to travel halfway up England with the money and then see god knows who when we got off. That didn't leave us in a strong position at all. Warby said we should leave it at the left luggage at the station. I hadn't got that far. I was still travelling up by train and the world watching me.

But it did mean – if the circus was OK – that we were in business fair and square. Like the Mafia in America, Eddie told us, they get out of crime by buying into firms. Lorry firms, meat, packing firms, casinos. The old man a big crook and the kids grow up nice and respectable. With clean money.

If we ever got that far. Suppose the circus was just a rag bag of animals that someone saw the chance to offload onto a couple of kids? It's all very well for Warby to be training lions already but there's more to business than that. The way he just nibbled out of Eddie's hand when he said 'circus'. All I could see were problems.

It was blowy and overcast when I got back to the flats. There was a smell of pee on the stairs and someone had spray painted their name a hundred times on the lift door. I still didn't have my key so I fiddled around with my bedroom window and climbed in. I left my new shirt on the bed and went into the kitchen.

I knew from the voice in the hall someone was there. A low voice, a familiar laugh. My stomach went tight. I thought of backing out, of leaving the flat. No one knew I was in yet.

I went in. Dad was sitting at the table with the chair back to front. His hair was slicked forward to hide his thinness at the front. Mum was also at the table drinking a cup of tea, she looked tired.

Dad gave me a broad smile. 'Hello, Davey.'

'Hello, Dad,' I said trying to look cheerful.

On the table was a number of packages in pretty paper. Dad handed me one.

I unwrapped it. It was a shirt. Exactly the same shirt I had just got from Eddie.

'You like it?'

'Yeh it's good. Thanks.'

Mum said, 'Did you have a good day?' She always asks that. One of those questions like how do you do, that it would never do to give the answer to. So she got the same one I always give.

'Alright.'

I couldn't tell her I've just seen Eddie and I'm bunking off again tomorrow. Could I?

She said, 'I've got some bad news.'

She was looking into her teacup. She seemed to be growing old even as I watched her. There's a photo of my mum just before she got married with a girlfriend in Spain. She was really a good looker. It's a colour picture, her hair long and dark brown, no grey in it. And a smile, a real smile – not one of those put on things for half a second, but like she was really enjoying herself.

'I got laid off today,' Mum said. She looked up at me and sighed. 'I hoped it was going to last, this job.'

Dad said, 'There's other jobs.'

'There aren't,' she said.

'Well,' he said, 'that's where my money'll come in useful.'

'What you doing, Dad?'

He said, 'I got a job with an importers. Clothing. Local. You know that ted in the market? I'm working with him.'

That accounted for the shirt. I had a butterflies feeling. I wondered whether Eddie had told him anything.

'Your father's coming back,' Mum said. That hit me smack. Change and change about. Just as you got used to something – you got shook up like flakes in a snowstorm. If I wasn't so big I could have bawled. Not again.

'We're going to give it another try,' said Dad. He was holding her hand on the table, and gently massaging her palm. It seemed like a dead jellyfish, she had taken her life completely out of it.

I couldn't understand. She didn't look happy.

Nothing like that picture. More like a dummy in a waxworks with a taped voice behind.

Mum said, 'Kathy and you will have to share from tonight.'

Another bombshell. Kathy shared with Mum and if Dad moved . . .

'It's too small,' I said weakly.

Dad put his hand on mine. 'It won't be for long. This is a good job. It's got prospects. I'll have us out of here. Don't you worry about that, son.'

I wasn't worried about him getting us out of here. I was worried about him. But more than him for the moment I was worried about the money. If Kathy was moving into my room what was I going to do with it? Tonight.

Dad got up. 'Another cup of tea, anyone?'

Mum shook her head. I said, 'OK, I'll just put this shirt away.'

I left the kitchen. In the hallway it was like coming out of a scorching hot day into a rain shower. I stood against the door breathing the cooler air.

I heard Dad say, 'He's a bit upset, but I'll make it up to him.'

I went into the bedroom and looked at the two shirts. Yes identical, down to the label. I put them both away in the built-in cupboard.

Then I panicked. The money! It can't stay here. Warby's got to have it. I got a suitcase out of the cupboard and opened it. I would just chuck the bag in and run round with the suitcase.

Except I couldn't, because the money wasn't there.

I ran round to Warby's empty-handed but my head was boiling over.

18

Warby's big brother Rick answered the door. He was in his vest with a towel over his shoulder. He called into the flat which smelt of frying. His mother came out and said Warby was having his tea but I could come in and wait.

Warby was in the sitting room eating at the table. His dad was seated in an armchair watching the news on TV and mopping egg up with bread. In a high chair was Natasha with food round her face, waving a spoon. Rick was ironing a shirt.

Warby was eating egg and chips. Leaning on the plate was a slice of white bread and a big mug of tea. Warby pulled a chunk off the bread and began to mop up his egg just like his dad. Both had their heads down wiping their plates.

His mum said, 'Would you like a cup of tea?'

'Yes please,' I said shyly. I'd been here before but I didn't know any of them well and I wanted to get Warby out.

She poured me out a cup of tea and gave me a couple of biscuits. The room was untidier than our house. It had a musty, grease under things smell. Warby's mum was a dinner lady but not at our school. His dad was unemployed and Rick was a trainee electrician.

She said, 'How's your mother? I haven't seen her in a while.'

I said, 'She's fine.' Although I knew she wasn't. I couldn't say my dad's back in front of everyone.

She said, 'Rick, don't come in drunk tonight.'

Rick sighed but didn't reply.

His dad turned. 'You heard your mother. Why don't you reply to your mother?'

'I wasn't drunk,' said Rick, his head down, concentrating on his ironing.

'Three in the morning you woke the baby last night,' said Warby's mum.

Natasha had her fingers in the bowl of food and was wiping it on her face.

'You'll lose that job,' his dad said.

Rick picked his shirt off the ironing board and strode out of the room.

'What can you do with him?' said his mother, cleaning up the baby.

Warby indicated with his eyes that this was a regular show.

'Thinks jobs grows on trees,' said his dad picking up a paper, then turned to Warby. 'Don't you take after him.'

I mouthed to Warby 'come on'. He mouthed back 'what's up?' I couldn't tell him in a couple of words. I just shook my fists and gritted my teeth.

Warby swilled down the tea. He got up. 'Just going out for a while, Mum.'

'Then you can take your sister.'

'Oh Mum.'

'Don't oh Mum me. She's been in all day. Your father won't take her out. His nibs is out on the town and I've got a pile of washing.'

'We wanna go and play cricket.'

She was taking Natasha out of the chair. 'Then she can watch.'

'I feel like a cissy.'

His mother didn't answer but went to clip Warby round the ear. He ducked and she missed.

As we walked out into the courtyard with the push-chair Warby was in a rotten mood. Pretty soon he was going to be in a worse one.

'Soon as I get the money I'm leaving,' he said.

'It's gone,' I said.

Warby stopped pushing the baby. 'What do you mean it's gone?'

'It's not under my bed anymore.'

'Can't be gone. You sure that's where you put it?'

'Yes.'

Warby was frowning, his blue eyes screwed up. 'Maybe you moved it in your sleep.'

'It's nowhere in the room. Someone's taken it.'

Natasha began to cry. Warby started walking again. She stopped.

'Who?' said Warby leaning on the handles and screwing up his face. You could always see Warby thinking. He punched into his fist. 'It has to be either an inside or an outside job.'

I had a sudden thought. 'Oh God.'

'What's up?'

'My window's been open for the last couple of days. Cuz I lost my key.'

Warby kicked the pushchair. The baby began crying.

'Oh shut up,' he said to the baby, otherwise ignoring her. 'You realize we've lost that circus?'

'Eddie!'

'I was going to learn to train lions,' he said morosely.

I said, 'Eddie took it.'

Warby looked up at me.

I went on. 'He sent someone round while he was talking to us.'

Warby stiffened. 'Let's go see him.' He began pushing the chair again. Natasha subsided.

'He won't admit it,' I said following after.

Warby was gripping the pram handle tightly and striding along. I had an effort to keep up.

'It's no good just going up to him and asking him if he stole our money. He'll say he didn't.'

'But we know he did,' said Warby still pushing on.

'Stop.' I gripped the chair, Warby pushed on, but the chair was undecided. It tipped. Fortunately Natasha was strapped in. She began to cry. Warby put the chair right and stuck a dummy in the baby's mouth. She threw it out.

We were by the market which was deserted except for a dustcart and men collecting the rubbish. Where they'd been one half of the market was clean, as if it had been inside an invisible box that protected it from the rubbishy half. Ahead on the high street it was quiet. Only a couple of restaurants were open.

Suddenly there was a commotion on the high street. Two figures rushed out of a cafe and were running towards us. The cafe door swung a second time and two men shouted after them.

It was only after they had been running a little way I recognized them as Kathy and Sue. They ran out of the high street and into the market square. Kathy was ahead with Sue running after. The two men from the cafe began to give chase. By the time they arrived at the market the girls were hidden by the dustcart. The two men stood on the corner undecided, waved their arms and turned back.

We rapidly crossed the market and turned into the flats. I caught Sue's head on a first floor landing.

'They're gone,' I called up.

The two girls stood up and looked over.

'I got something for you,' called Warby, waving them down.

'What?'

'Something you'll like.' He had a secret smile.

The two girls ran down the stairs. When they got to us they were breathy and red-faced.

'Give it back,' said Warby leaning low on the push-chair handle.

Kathy open-mouthed looked to Sue, who looked quickly away from me.

'I don't know what you're talking about,' said Kathy.

'Don't give me that,' said Warby. 'You took it.'

Kathy smiled, and traced a circle with her foot. 'So what if we did?'

'We want it back,' said Warby.

Sue said, 'Hark at big chief here. It don't belong to you.'

'Nor you,' said Warby.

'It belongs to whoever has got it,' said Kathy.

By which time I'd caught up. Kathy and Sue had taken the money and Warby had guessed. They'd been going through the same fuss in the cafe as we had in the camera shop.

Warby said, 'It's no good to you.'

'Nor you,' said Kathy.

'But it is,' I joined in. 'We got a deal going.'

I told them about the circus.

Kathy looked at Sue and said in her coolest voice. 'Fancy a circus, Sue?'

How I hated her! Our idea, our money, our circus. She always did that. Kathy got everything. Now she had our dream in her hands. I could sense she was going to drop it and squash it with her foot.

Sue said, 'Circuses are for kids. They're cruel to animals.'

Warby said to the girls, 'Look after Tash for a minute,' and he pushed me backwards. When we were out of earshot he said in a low voice, 'We've got to bring them in on it.'

'No,' I protested, tears of rage welling up.

Warby shrugged. 'It's that or nothing.'

'Nothing,' I said and began to walk off. I wanted Warby to follow but I couldn't look back. I walked away from them all and begged Warby to come with me. But he didn't. When I turned the corner of the flats I ran. I ran with rage, I ran with the tears flowing. I was miserable and angry at once. If there had been anything to break I would have broken it. I wanted to smash the world with a hammer. Then smash each bit to powder and smash the powder to atoms. Smash everything.

I had run to the railway. I climbed the fence and in my rush and anger I scraped my hand at the top. Astride the fence I sucked the blood. By the time I had dropped to the ground all the anger had gone and I was left simply with misery. I began to cry.

In the dark of the hut I let the tears run. I lay flat out on the boards and let everything pour into my hurt. I didn't want Kathy to have it and I couldn't stop Kathy having it. I wanted my mum here, singing over me, but my mum was with my dad. And everything went bung with my dad.

It came at me; the whole of that afternoon, like someone had just been through my head with a food mixer and I was lying in the puddle on the dark floor.

The door opened. I opened an eye – Warby was standing there, a shadow against the sunlight. I sat up and pulled my knees up. I knew in the dark he couldn't see my tears.

He said, 'I had to Shorty. There was nothing else to do.' He sat down on the box nearest me and put a hand on my shoulder. 'But I said it had to be you too.'

A train was coming. I could feel its 'had to be you' through the boards. It burst out of the long tunnel and rattled past. Had to be you, had to be you, had to be you too.

As it died off Warby said, 'We're all going up to Leeds tomorrow.'

19

'Come on, Davey.'

A voice somewhere. My body was stiff through restless sleep. I had lain in bed and waited for Dad to come back. For the pubs to shut and the front door to bang and a clumsy walk down the hallway. And the row that would follow.

I thought if I closed my eyes the door would bang . . . Every noise outside caused me to listen. The footfalls on the landings, the closing of doors, the squeaks and creaks of the night. I listened to them all.

And he didn't come.

It was already growing light when I slept.

'Come on, Davey.'

Kathy was shaking me. I groaned and opened my eyes to see her fully dressed over me. She was wearing her school things.

'We gotta pack.'

I sat up. She got out a suitcase and put it on my bed. There were two beds in the room. I remembered she had moved in.

'You know Dad didn't come home,' I said.

'Creep,' she said, 'I moved for nothing.'

She packed a towel and a swimming costume.

'What's that for?'

'Leeds is near the sea.'

Was it? I scratched my head. Maybe it was. I looked at the clock. Six-fifteen!

'Why so early?'

'Mum's lost her job. Remember?'

Now it made sense. Mum wouldn't be off to work. We couldn't pack with her around. I threw the blankets off.

'How we getting our stuff out?'

'Pack now,' she said, 'then I'll hide it in the pram shed. Then we make out we're off to school.'

Without dressing – I was shy in front of my sister – I sorted out some clothes to take up. A towel for the beach, my trunks, a shirt, change of socks and pants and a sweater in case it got cold. Kathy saw me and started sorting out some dresses and shoes.

'What are they for?'

She sniffed. 'You gotta look good to do business.'

'That dress is from a jumble.'

'Never was.'

'Was.'

'Prove it.'

I shrugged. Didn't really care but knew it annoyed her. I watched her packing; two pairs of shoes and two dresses. No skin off my nose, long as I didn't do all the carrying.

'What about the washing stuff?' I said.

Kathy bit her thumb, then shook her head. 'Can't take our toothbrushes, Mum might notice. We can buy

99

a bar of soap. And I don't 'spose our teeth will fall out if we miss one night.'

Quietly she climbed onto my bed and opened the bedroom window. She climbed out onto the landing. I passed out the case. It was a fair weight with all her stuff. She tiptoed along the landing.

In a few minutes she returned.

We decided to go back to bed.

We got up late. Mum pushed us around. Both of us had overslept and we seemed to be forever queueing behind each other. For the bathroom, for the cereal, for the toilet.

Kathy said, 'Where's Dad?'

Mum said, 'I don't know' in such a cold voice that we knew better than to push it.

'What you going to do?' said Kathy.

'I'm going to get an injunction,' she said.

I didn't know exactly what it was but I knew it was something to do with the police and keeping Dad out. The women in the hostel kept talking about injunctions.

Mum had lit a cigarette. She had a worried, nervy look. She saw me looking at her and gave me a weak smile.

She said, 'If I'm back late tonight don't worry.'

What could we say to that when we weren't going to be back at all?

We took up our school bags and left.

On the landing I said, 'What's going on with Dad?'

'She don't want him but she's scared to tell him,' Kathy said.

'So where is he?'

Kathy shrugged.

At the bottom of the stairs we crammed our school bags into our suitcase. I was closing it up when Warby came. He hadn't brought anything!

'It's only one night,' he scoffed.

'Aren't you going in the sea then?'

Warby said he hadn't realized Leeds was by the sea. He ran back to his house and brought back his swimming things. Sue still hadn't arrived. And she had the money.

Kathy said she would go and call for her, and left us. I wasn't too happy. Had they planned this? Warby said he didn't think so. It seemed too smart waking me up to pack.

We waited several minutes and then headed towards Sue's flat. And met her and Kathy coming towards us. Sue was struggling with a suitcase, and a shoulder bag.

'I couldn't get out. My brother and my sister were everywhere.'

Warby had run into the road, and stopped a taxi. The driver was a grouchy man with a walrus moustache and cloth cap. He wouldn't let us get in until Warby showed him a £20 note.

'Mind you keep your feet off the seats,' he growled as we got in.

At last we would get away from the flats.

Not so easily. We pulled round the corner and met the traffic crawling along the main road. Jimmy came past and waved. For quite a way he was able to follow us.

'Gis a lift,' he called.

Joe joined him. They were both calling to us with the taxi stuck in the traffic.

We didn't know what to do. If we ignored them they would just make a fuss. If we talked to them it would just draw attention to us. Then we saw Mr Kershaw on his bicycle. He was coming up the inside. We ducked down and waited.

The driver turned his head. 'Oi, you want to muck about – you walk!'

There was a tap on the window. We looked up. There was Mr Kershaw peering through the window. His red woolly hat made me want to laugh. The girls did.

Warby opened the window.

'What are you all doing on the floor?'

'We lost a pound, sir.'

He looked at us all and frowned. 'What are you doing in a taxi?'

'Going on holiday,' said Sue.

'I hope you have permission.'

'Yes sir,' we all said.

Mr Kershaw gave us a searching look. He caught my eye, I looked away. Finally he said, 'I hope you have the holiday you deserve.'

We said we would and he cycled off.

We drew ourselves back on the seats. Kathy started to say something but Warby put a finger to his lips and indicated the driver who seemed to have an ear twisted in our direction. We giggled secretly to each other as the traffic began to speed up and we left our part of town.

20

Everyone looked so normal. We must've looked normal – I think – and yet we had a suitcase full of money. That made me wonder about the others. What they had in their bags. Bombs, guns. You wouldn't know. Maybe that man in the bowler hat had just murdered his wife. You just don't know what they've been up to. Why they're here, who they're meeting. That woman in the blue skirt – maybe she's a spy. Why not? Stations are the perfect place to meet. So many people. So many spies. So many suitcases full of money.

Warby joined us in the station hall after paying the taxi.

'There's not enough left for the train fare,' he said.

Kathy sighed with exasperation as if she expected us to make a mess of it.

'You'll have to get some out of the case,' Warby said.

'What 'ere?' exclaimed Kathy.

Sue took her arm. 'Let's go to the loo.'

'Hang about,' I said.

'Why, you got the cash?' said Kathy.

'I don't trust you.'

'Here you are,' said Sue, holding out her suitcase, 'you get it.'

I hesitated, looking to Warby.

'Oh leave 'em,' he said. 'Just hurry up about it.'

Kathy blew him a kiss as the girls went off arm in arm. 'See ya in Hollywood.'

Warby called to the girls, 'Meet you in the cafeteria.' He pointed.

They nodded.

Above the platform entrances was the board giving the platforms and the train times. It was very confusing with so many. We wandered up and down looking at each one.

'That's it,' I exclaimed, 'leaves in twenty minutes from platform seven. Change at Doncaster.'

It had a buffet car. We decided we'd have a slap-up lunch. The works. The girls could pay for it. If anyone was suspicious we'd say – it's their money!

We went into the cafeteria. Warby picked up a tray. 'I'll get the food. Put my gear in your case, will ya?'

'It already weighs a ton.'

'Towel and cossy won't make any difference.'

I reluctantly took his stuff while he joined the queue. I opened the case and my bag and Kathy's underwear fell out. I heard a laugh behind me and went prickly round the neck. I shoved it all back, jammed in Warby's and closed up.

There was one empty table. I went for it and put my case on a chair. The table was covered in dirty crockery. I find that really offputting, people's mess. Lipstick round a cup, a smell of grease and vinegar, egg yellow.

I grabbed a tray and piled it all on. The smell of it turned my stomach. It's like looking into someone's mouth when they're eating.

Warby joined me at the table.

'I'll be glad when we're there,' I said.

'Me too,' said Warby, sorting out the creamiest cake.

I took my pick. That left a couple of dry-looking ring doughnuts for the girls.

'Wonder what this circus owner is like?'

'Probably Italian,' said Warby. 'Doubles up as ring-master,' he added with a mouthful of cream. 'I bet ya. You ask him.'

I suddenly felt tired. It came out of nowhere. My eyes were blinking and I could feel myself nodding in the chair. I'd sleep on the train. Couple of hours, put a bit in the bank. I yawned.

Warby said, 'I'm just going to have a look out for the girls.'

My chin rocked onto my chest. In the background I could hear the noise of the station but it seemed far away. There was an announcement – a train stopping at lots of places, leaving shortly from platform fifteen . . .

Warby was shaking me.

'What's up?'

He looked very angry. 'I just saw the girls get on the train.'

And I was angry too. What a dirty trick. They were going to leave us here.

We ran to the ticket offices. There was a queue at all of them. Warby lined up. By the clock there were three minutes.

'Get in another queue,' said Warby. 'First one there takes the money.'

My queue seemed to be moving quite quickly. Then it stopped. A young American couple were asking lots of questions. They didn't seem to know where they wanted to go. They were asking the ticket man and then asking the prices and about hotels – then discussing it between them. At last they got their credit cards out and couldn't decide which one to use.

Warby's line had caught up with mine. Then he was at the front. I got out of line and joined Warby. The two Americans were chatting away as if the ticket man was a long-lost cousin.

Warby didn't have enough for two to Leeds. He didn't know what to say. He was about to walk away from the office.

'Two to Doncaster,' I came in with.

We just had enough for that. The time on the clock was the leaving time. We ran like crazy. I was holding the suitcase in both arms in front of me. Warby raced ahead.

He had the tickets. I suddenly panicked when I thought he'll leave me too. I stumbled on, the case getting heavier and heavier. I knew this would happen. I knew I'd get stuck with it.

I stopped in a lather. The case was too heavy. I put it down, picked it up again and lumbered on.

Warby was standing by the platform entrance. The train was pulling out of the station.

21

We sagged like a pair of burst footballs. There goes the money, there goes the circus. It was impossible to believe. The way we had set off this morning, singing along in the taxi.

But the platform was empty. We could not bring the train back.

Warby whined, 'If only we had bought the tickets first.'

'We couldn't. We didn't have enough money.'

Warby kicked my suitcase. 'We found the money then we lost it again.'

We couldn't move from the spot. Like a bird that couldn't leave its dead mate we couldn't believe it. Sue, my sister and all the money.

'It's gone,' Warby moaned. 'Gone.'

Like an old man who'd dropped his false teeth down a well.

'Cup of tea?' I said. Don't know why. I didn't want one.

Warby shook his head. Here it had happened. Here he would die.

The board was changing. It went blank and then

flicked up the next train. Newcastle in twenty minutes. The barrier was being opened again by a ginger-haired railway man in thick glasses.

He said, 'You'll have to clear that area.'

We didn't move.

'What's up, lost a fiver?'

Warby let out a long sigh. It must've caught the train.

'We missed our train to Doncaster.'

'My sister's on it,' I said.

The main smiled, showing a gold tooth. 'There's more than one train you know.'

Warby jumped up. 'Is there . . . is there another one to Doncaster?'

The man nodded. 'There's a train to Edinburgh. Only makes a couple of stops. Might even catch that train up. Platform ten.' He looked at his watch. 'Leaving in a couple of minutes.'

We thanked him as if he had saved our lives and ran.

The train was in the platform. It was going to Doncaster! That's where the girls changed, that's where we'd catch them. We got quickly through the barrier and climbed in the first carriage. We weren't going to take any chances this time.

The carriage was busy. Not packed but crowded enough so that we'd have to sit with other people. We decided to go further down the train. From what we'd seen of it from the platform it had lots of carriages.

We made our way down the aisle of the carriages, me in front with the suitcase. There were people coming towards us. Maybe it was crowded down that end too? We stood aside for them and then continued. We went through the connecting doors into the second carriage. There were a few more free seats. Should we take this or try the next?

We went onto the third. Not any better than the one before. We spotted an empty section and made for it. Sat down opposite each other in the window seats and stretched out.

I was still in a rage at my sister, at the same time relieved. At least we wouldn't have to travel up with the money and have a cold panic every time someone looked at us.

A large man with a spotty face stopped, looked the space over and sat down next to Warby. He took over half the seat and squeezed Warby into the window. Why did he have to pick us? There was more room for him somewhere else. I could see Warby wasn't pleased. We'd move when the train started.

He had a cloth bag which he put on the floor. He took out a newspaper from it and began to read. He was wearing a pair of grubby jeans and a T-shirt. The T-shirt had a couple of tomatoes on it with words I couldn't make out behind the paper. I strained to look and caught a cold look. But I caught the words too. 'Don't Squeeze me till I'm Yours.'

His hair was really short, so short it stood stiff like the bristles on a brush. But it was the spots on his face that interested me. So many of them; pink and squashed, like craters on the moon. I know it's rude to stare and he couldn't help it but I'd never seen so many spots in one place.

He caught me looking at him again. His deep eyes

burnt into me like torches, his thin mouth seemed about to spit. I turned away and wanted to move badly.

I looked out of the window at the people hurrying down the train with suitcases. Beyond them another train had just pulled in. Doors were opening and banging and the people pouring out. What a rush the world was in.

Where did they have to go so fast? One man in a suit was sprinting down the platform as if there were a prize for the first through the barrier. He seemed to set off a panic; the others began to worry that the gates would be shut on them and began to race after. Maybe there was more than one prize.

Our train had begun to move slowly. Warby looked at me and smiled. I smiled back. We were off. Up the map of England to beat Kathy and Sue to Doncaster.

I looked at the spotty man. He was staring at me. I felt uncomfortable and turned to the window. The train had already got to speed. This one was certainly not going to hang about anywhere. We passed a local train as if it were standing still. The people in it reading or staring at us as we went flashing past. Our only meeting and most of 'em weren't looking.

I turned, the spotty man was still staring at me. I couldn't take it. It was as if he were searching me, scouring out my thoughts. I thought for an instant he can mind read. Those eyes were pinpointing my thoughts.

I mustn't think of the money. I mustn't think of the quarter of a million pounds in £20 notes that we had found in the derelict building and we were now going to buy a circus with. His eyes knew what I mustn't think.

'Got any money?' I said quietly to Warby.

He took out a handful of change. 'That's the lot.'

I took it. 'Just going to get some drinks.'

I had to get away from those eyes. Maybe the train was emptier further down.

I got into the next carriage. It was about as full as our own. Down the end there was an empty group. I went a little closer. And stopped.

Just over the empty seats, in the seats behind, head into a newspaper was my dad. I turned in panic and ran back to our carriage.

When I had sat down Warby said, 'No drinks?'

I shook my head. The spotty man was staring at me. I didn't want to go into explanations with him watching. I stared out the window. Back gardens rushing by. Fences, extensions, washing and patches of grass. And windows, windows like eyes, watching, passing messages so that each house knew who to look out for.

My dad! Suppose he should come this way, what would I say to him? How would I explain what I was doing on the train?

Stories jumbled in my head. A holiday, a school trip. I must pray that he didn't move. I hated Kathy more than ever. If we'd have been on the train with her this wouldn't have happened.

A ticket collector was coming down punching tickets. Warby was searching his pockets. The collector was standing over us. Warby was going through each pocket in turn, his face had gone a bright red. He looked exactly like he was about to cheat the trains.

'Got it somewhere,' he mumbled. I had found mine and showed it to the collector. He snipped it and handed it back. Warby had started again going through his pockets.

'We bought them both together,' I said.

The collector sniffed. His big nose twisted. He'd heard every story a hundred times.

Warby stopped, face flushed, pockets turned out. 'Can't find it,' he said weakly.

The man sighed. 'Where you going?' He got out his book.

'Doncaster.'

'Where d'you live?'

'London.'

'Name and address.'

Warby gave him the details. The whole carriage was watching. I put my ticket away and felt a piece of card. I pulled it out. It was Warby's ticket.

I handed it over. The ticket man's eyes rolled upwards. He ripped up his page, clipped the ticket and moved on.

Warby shook his fist at me, gritted his teeth as if he would rip me apart. I said sorry. He carried on growling at me.

I looked out of the window. I couldn't care what Warby thought with my dad in the next carriage. All he had to do was stretch his legs in this direction . . . I had to move.

I stood up and went to get the suitcase.

'I'm going to the next carriage.'

Warby looked at me, puzzled. 'What for?'

Without replying I took down the case and headed up the train. Once in the next carriage I stopped and waited. Warby was following.

'You're going the wrong way,' he said.

I shook my head. 'My dad's on the train.'

'You're kidding!'

I pointed. 'Two carriages up.'

Warby looked behind him, as if he could see that far. 'What's he doing on the train?'

I shrugged. What did I ever know about my dad.

Warby said, 'We'd better go right to the back.'

We carried on, into the more crowded carriage at the back of the train that we'd come through when we'd got on. We found a couple of seats opposite each other in the aisle. I loaded my case in the rack and we sat down.

I leaned forward and said quietly, 'I want to get off next stop.'

Warby shook his head. 'Then we'll never catch your sister.'

I looked down the train. He could come through and there was nowhere for me to go. No more carriages, just the track beyond. I imagined jumping, and running flat out as I hit the ground to counteract the speed of the train, like I'd seen in a film. Not at this speed. It'd be like throwing an egg against a wall.

And then he was coming. Down the carriage in exactly the way I dreaded. I pulled my head in and turned to face the window, hoping he would not see me.

'Hello, Davey boy.' His voice rang in surprise. 'What you doing here?'

He was standing over me. I looked up at him, he was smiling.

'Hello, Dad.'

Warby cut in. 'We're on a geography trip, Mr Roberts.'

'That's nice.' He was still smiling. I didn't know what to say to him.

He said, 'How long you going for?'

'Just a couple of days,' said Warby.

He was still smiling but he looked awkward up there. There wasn't room for him to sit. He looked up and down the carriage and rubbed his forehead.

'Why don't you kids come and join me. Eh?'

It wasn't possible to refuse. I took down the suitcase and then Dad took it off me and we followed him down the train. Through the carriage where we had sat previously, where the spotty man sat and now stared at us as we passed, and on to the next carriage.

Dad put the case up on the rack and we sat down again. Warby and me had window seats across a table. My dad sat next to me.

He said, 'I'm gong off to get some food. Keep my place.'

He went off.

'He's not so bad,' said Warby.

I twisted in my seat. What did Warby know about my dad? But then what did I know? I began to wonder what he was doing on the train. Why hadn't he come home last night? What did he do when he wasn't with us?

I looked out of the window. I imagined myself a giant jumping hedges at the speed of the train. Up and over keeping up with the express. I jumped a river and up a hill. Now I disappeared from view as the train went through a cutting. There I was on the ridge, striding over the hilltops, my head in the sky.

Dad returned with an armful of drinks, sandwiches and cakes. He gave us a can each. Then sorted the rest out, spreading them out on the table before us.

I said, 'Where are you going, Dad?'

He said, 'I'll be back home tonight. Just some business.' He looked at me uncomfortably and then looked down at his hands. 'I haven't been much of a father, have I?'

I didn't reply. I couldn't.

'We married very young, me and your mum. Neither of us were ready for it.' He looked up and gave me a short grin. 'I never know what you're thinking.'

What could I say to him?

'Maybe it's because we never talked,' he said. He swallowed. 'We don't know each other that well do we?' He turned to look out the window. I could see a tear in the corner of his eye. 'Funny meeting like this.'

I wished the train was empty. It was embarrassing Warby being here.

He said, 'Remember that holiday we had in Broadstairs?'

I could just remember us all sitting on a beach together.

'We were a family then.'

He wiped his eyes with the back of his hand. 'Your mother . . . she doesn't make it easy for me.'

These waters were too deep. I was sinking and swirling in his emotion.

He licked a lip. 'I thought maybe if . . . ' He hesitated and began again. 'I wonder if she's right for you. Maybe if you lived with me?' He was looking at me intensely, his eyes still wet. 'Would you like that, Davey?'

How could I answer him? He only wanted one reply.

'Would you like to give it a try?'

Oh God take me away. Put me anywhere else. Stop these questions.

'I 'spose it's a bit sudden for you. Think about it. Me and you. Kathy can stay with your mum. You'll still be able to go and see her. Me and you.'

I thought in horror he's just come back to get me. I thought that's why he's on this train. He has come to take me with him.

'Don't you want that drink?'

I took a sip.

He said, 'Whatever I've done, whatever I do I love you.'

He held my face between his hands, his lip trembling. I felt captured, as if he could squeeze me like pastry.

'I've been a beast, Davey. Your mother knows that. Some of the things I put her through . . . ' He sniffed and was suddenly crying. His body heaving, his face sunk onto his hands and loud sobs.

I looked at Warby. Warby was embarrassed. I'd never seen a grown man crying before. An elderly man and woman in the seats across the aisle were staring at us.

Dad suddenly got up and strode rapidly down the train and disappeared into the next carriage. I looked out of the window and wished I could jump through and out, over that duck pond and away.

In a few minutes he returned. He had stopped crying and his face had that shiny just-washed look. He grinned as he sat down, took my hand and gave it a squeeze.

Dad was caught in his own thought and although he held my hand he no longer looked at me. After a while it was as if he had forgotten I was with him.

The landscape had changed. We were entering a large city. Oblong windowless factories, railway wagons full of cement, tired houses with pocket-size gardens. Like a kid's lego set with everything pushed together.

Dad suddenly stood up. 'Come with me,' he indicated to both of us. He began to walk away. I looked to Warby. He shrugged and we both followed obediently.

Between the two carriages he stopped and drew me close to him. 'Think about what I said.'

I nodded.

He took out his wallet and took out a couple of £5 notes. He gave us one each.

'For your trip.'

The train was drawing into a station. In the carriage people were lifting down cases and coming towards the doors.

Dad said, 'I'm getting off here. Don't forget. Me and you. No matter what happens. Me and you.'

The train had stopped. A lot of people were bustling around us. Dad pulled me to him and hugged me.

'We can beat 'em.' With a squeeze of my shoulder, a final sigh, he turned and got off the train.

I was a washed rag, twisted dry. I couldn't think anymore.

We went back to our seats and neither of us spoke. I still wanted to run but heaven knows where to. I sunk into the seat and watched the train pull out. Dad always did this to me. Came back just as you had got used to him not being around. When he was in prison that time. Did he really mean me to go and live with him?

Warby tapped me on the shoulder. I was glad he was with me. He said, 'I think your suitcase has gone.'

22

Warby looked about him scratching his head; Doncaster. He looked to me. How could I help? I'd never been to Doncaster before. It might as well have said Moon station. He went to a railman who pointed up at a couple of video screens. Me and Warby tried to make sense of them, all those towns we'd never heard of, and having to change times like 14.29 to everyday times. The third one down was a London to Newcastle train, arriving in fourteen minutes on this platform. I thought that must be the girls' train. Warby wasn't sure. I insisted it had to be – what else was coming up from London? But Warby kept saying – what about the other trains? I pointed them out to him – how could the girls be on those? He said maybe they didn't call it the London train anymore. I started explaining again when suddenly Warby started laughing – and I could see he'd been playing me up. I wanted to punch him on the nose.

'You're easier to wind up than a yoyo!'

When I'd calmed down, we sat down on a bench to wait for the train Kathy and Sue were on. Warby was in a perky mood which was good for me. I didn't want to think about what had been happening and that was just as well because Warby wouldn't let me. We started by playing smashing fists and both got very raw knuckles. Then we played the game where one of us picks a person on the station and the other one has to guess what crime they've committed. Warby picked a vicar and he'd just stolen six packets of bacon from the supermarket. I picked a smart-looking air hostess who'd just forged her post office book.

An announcement came through. We strained our ears. I caught the platform number and a list of strange towns. The train from London was due any minute on this platform.

I punched Warby on the shoulder. 'See! See! '

Along the platform people, including our bacon thief and forger, picked up luggage and moved to the platform edge. There was another announcement. A local train to Leeds was due across the bridge.

'Come on,' said Warby, 'we'll wait on that platform.'

'What's the point?' I exclaimed as he pulled me from the seat just as the London train was drawing in.

'The art of surprise,' he yelled as we ran over the bridge and down the steps. A huge reel of electrical cable was lying a little way down the platform. Warby pulled me in behind it.

The local train came in on the platform we were now on. Doors swung and banged as people began to get on and off, or stood around wondering what to do. Some made for the bridge. There was an announcement and those standing about picked up their cases and headed for the stairs. From the other platform people began coming down. From either train people were rushing to make their connection.

All the coming and going got me nervous. Suppose we missed 'em? Then we wouldn't know whether they'd stayed on the train or headed back to London.

'Suppose they've been arrested?' I whispered.

'Suppose they've been swallowed by a whale. If they're going to Leeds they've got to catch this one. Right?'

'*If* they're going to Leeds . . . ' I said.

'What d'you mean?' exclaimed Warby, rounding on me.

'You never know with my sister. That's all.'

'Your whole family is crackers!' he hissed.

The rush was over. The mainline train was pulling out, although the local didn't seem in much of a hurry. There were no more people going up the steps and just one or two coming down. Then no one. Sue and Kathy hadn't got off.

I felt like I'd swallowed a lump of lead. Warby kicked the wall behind him.

'They've made fools of us,' he yelled.

I was annoyed at Warby for saying what I felt. Like he'd made it happen by coming across the bridge. I wanted to blame somebody.

Warby said, 'It was all your fault.'

'Why mine?' Warby was really cheesing me off.

'You should've have hidden it properly in your room.'

'Stuff yourself.'

'She ain't my sister.'

'How can I help that?' He was really working me up.

'First your flaming sister, then your flaming dad turns up. Next thing we'll have your uncle and aunts and all your cousins.'

'You could pickle onions in your mouth.'

Warby grabbed me, I ducked away – but he just pulled me in behind the reel.

'Shut up!' he exclaimed and pointed.

There were the girls on the platform opposite, just coming out the Ladies. Sue was struggling with the suitcase, holding the handle with both hands and Kathy walking and waiting as if she were out with a dog.

They began to go up the stairs. We huddled in close watching their every move, waiting to spring our ambush. Warby looked at me and chuckled. He punched me lightly on the shoulder.

The girls were now off the bridge and walking towards the first carriages. Warby rushed out and shrieked.

The two girls jumped in fright. Sue dropped the case and Warby sat on it. I immediately joined him.

We sat there smiling up at the surprised girls. It almost made up for the aggravation they'd given us to see their faces. The two of them flapping like penguins. My sister's mouth open, Sue saying 'What what?' over and over, unable to come out with a question with any sense to it. We sat tight on the money and smiled sweetly at them.

Kathy finally said, 'What you doing here?'

'Waiting for you,' said Warby, matter of fact.

'How?' said Sue.

Warby shrugged. 'One minute we were at King's Cross and then the next we were here.' He looked to me. 'Must've been a time warp.'

I nodded.

Kathy said, 'Shall I call you Warpy then?' She was recovering quickly.

Warby pretended he hadn't heard.

Sue said, 'We'll miss the train.' Indicating the one still on the platform.

'You catch it,' said Warby.

Nobody moved.

'We're not going anywhere without that,' said Kathy, indicating the suitcase.

'Well,' said Warby rising, 'I'm going to get a drink. Coming Shorty?'

We took up the case and headed back over the foot-bridge. The girls followed at a distance scowling at us. When we were halfway over the bridge the local train pulled out.

In the foyer of the station was a cafe. I found a table and sat there with the suitcase wedged between me and the wall. The girls went to the counter to get some food.

When we were all sitting down Kathy said between mouthfuls of eggs and beans, 'We never thought you'd miss the train.'

Sue said, 'We just meant to panic you.'

Warby sneered. 'We don't panic that easy.'

I said, 'It was lucky there was another train.' Even as I said the words I was thinking if meeting Dad on the train is lucky then what's bad luck?

Warby told them about seeing Dad. Then Kathy quizzed me and I had to put her in the picture. I missed out the bit with Dad crying and I didn't say anything about him wanting me to live with him. I told them about the suitcase going.

Kathy didn't seem any more worried about the things in it than I was. I know Mum wouldn't like it but that was tomorrow and there were enough problems left in today to make tomorrow seem lifetimes away.

Sue went out and asked about the next Leeds train. It wasn't for a while so we all had some more drinks and a bit more food. Warby broke into the fiver Dad gave him.

We got onto knock knock jokes. Really corny stuff. Sue has this really loud laugh, sort of half hiccough and half dog bark. I knew everyone was looking at us. After a while I couldn't stand it and I got up to go to the loo. Warby shifted against the suitcase and I went back onto the platform. I could still hear Sue and I watched them all for a second through the window on the platform.

Like on TV. I could see how we were annoying the other people in the cafe. They were either looking at us in disapproval or trying hard not to look at us.

'Sue, Sue,' Kathy was shouting and hitting her over the head with a comic. Then Sue was laughing even more, putting it on, and I thought fancy travelling up by train with her.

When I came out of the toilet a train was in and people were getting off. Suddenly I stopped in my tracks. There was Dad coming out of a carriage carrying our suitcase!

I drew behind a pillar. Behind him followed Eddie and the spotty man.

They were obviously together. Just in case I had any doubts Eddie passed them both a cigarette. The spotty man, a lot taller than either of them, walked between them, making them seem like a peculiar family, with the father and two grown-up sons. They went up the steps of the footbridge and crossed to the other platform, just as the train they had got off pulled out.

I couldn't move now. It was stupid of me to wait. I should have taken my chance when they were in the middle of the footbridge. Now they sat on a bench almost opposite the pillar I was behind.

I hoped the others wouldn't come out.

Eddie and Dad were chatting, but they didn't look pleased. The spotty man got up and began to walk backwards and forwards along the platform. Dad had the suitcase between his knees and kept looking down the track.

It was obvious why they weren't happy. They hadn't come all this way to get a suitcase full of clothes. At some other time I would've enjoyed the joke.

Their train was coming. The three of them got up and went to the platform's edge as the train pulled in. At that moment the two girls and Warby came running out of the cafe. They saw me, waved and carried on running, Warby humping the case. They ran up the steps of the footbridge.

I dare not shout. I looked across the line. The three men were getting into the train. I waited until they were inside then sped after the others. I knew I might be seen but I had to risk it. I took the stairs of the bridge two at a time. The others were going down the other side. I had to catch them.

I was hit by a flurry of passengers and luggage. I fought my way through. They shouted and swore after me. I just pushed through. Down the stairs three at a time – there they were getting on the train. I jumped the last half a dozen steps and scrambled to my feet just as the whistle went. Kathy was standing at the train door calling. She seemed a hundred miles away.

The train began to pull away. I'd be left here on my own, without anybody or anything. I sprinted like crazy but the train was already picking up speed. Kathy was holding the door open. It was too fast, I was going to miss it. In a frantic effort I grasped her outstretched hand and got a foot onto the edge.

Kathy and Sue hauled me in.

23

Between the seats on my hands and knees I scowled at them.

'What a dirty trick!'

Warby and Kathy looked at each other.

'Don't give me that,' I spat at them as my panic died and my breath recovered.

'Give you what?' said Sue while Kathy indicated with a twirl of her fingers that I was screwy.

'You were going to leave me.'

'No we weren't,' said Warby crouching next to me. I pushed him away. He angrily pushed me back.

'The three of you were in it. You planned it in the cafe.'

Kathy put her hands on her hips. 'That's right, we were going to do a three-way carve-up,' bending to poke her face into mine.

Something blew in me. I stood up and went for the case up in the rack. I grasped the handle just as the three of them grasped me. I fought them punching and kicking. They got me down to the floor. Sue was sitting on my legs. Warby had his knees on my shoulders while Kathy sat on my stomach. I tried to lift my belly, I bit Warby on the knee. I screamed out, I yelled.

'Give in?' said Warby.

'No.' I twisted my head. There wasn't much else I could move. I was beaten and I wanted them to kill me.

Warby squeezed my nose. 'Give in.'

'Never,' I yelled through the pain.

'He won't,' said Kathy. 'You could beat him with a cricket bat and he wouldn't.'

'Too bad we haven't got any handcuffs,' said Sue. I could feel her tying my laces together.

Warby squeezed my nose again. 'Give in!'

I wriggled, I squirmed. I bashed my head on the floor.

'Get off him,' said Kathy. They all eased up, stood up and left me on the floor. I rolled over, shut my eyes, clenched my teeth. I wanted to jump out of the train, under the crashing wheels. I wanted to fill the hole in me with all my tears. But I wouldn't cry, not with them there. I couldn't let them see me cry.

The rumbling of the train seemed to be coming through me. I was a tunnel and the blackness curved and rolled as the train ran along the walls into the dark. The dark was the inside of me. Footsteps over me. Voices around me. I was shut in my dark.

Time passed and my misery became sulks. My pride was battered. I wanted them to talk to me and yet I knew I wouldn't listen if they tried. Finally I rose, tripped over the tied shoelaces, heard them giggle, slipped out of my shoes and without looking at any of them I walked a little way down the carriage and sat in an empty seat by the window.

What did I want now? Them to come and beg me. My best friend, my sister and her friend who were going to run out on me. Leave me nowhere while they ran off with the circus money. If I got the chance I would run off with it.

They didn't know about the others on the train. Why should I tell them?

I knew they were thinking about me. I was thinking about them but I would sit here like stone. Looking out the window, seeing only the light but nothing of the things that skipped past my eyes.

They came and sat next to me. Trying to be nice. They said sorry one after another. I looked out the window. They stayed and talked in whispers, not about me, but how it hurt when they laughed.

I wanted them to go, I wanted them to stay. I couldn't escape them now.

I turned and said, 'Must you follow me?'

''Fraid so,' said Warby with a smile and handed me a pair of shoes.

Kathy said, 'Do you like butter?' and held a paper buttercup under my chin.

'He's smiling. He's smiling,' called Sue in her crow's voice.

And I was.

It was a short-lived smile. Standing over us were Dad, the spotty man and Eddie.

'Hello kids,' said Eddie pleasantly. 'Got room for us.'
They all three sat down.

Kathy, Warby and Sue stiffened like tent pegs as they penned us in. Smiles went, they looked to each other helplessly. I watched it all from the window seat as if I were the stranger on the train.

Next to me were Kathy and Sue, opposite Warby squeezed in by Eddie and Dad. The spotty man, his legs cramped between the seats, pressed against Sue.

'Had a good journey?' asked Eddie, over-friendly.

'A bit bumpy,' said Warby in a flat voice.

'That's the new trains,' said Eddie. 'Inferior Suspension. Wouldn't you say, me old fruit?'

'What you doing here, Dad?' said Kathy darkly.

He was cleaning his fingernails with a broken match. Without looking up he said, 'I'm working for Eddie.'

'Who's Eddie working for?'

Eddie smiled and wiped back his hair. 'I've come to inform my former employers that I'm taking another job.'

'Come for your holiday pay?' said Kathy.

Eddie chuckled, and scratched the back of his ear. He looked to the spotty man who scowled and turned his head away.

Eddie said, 'May I introduce my associate, Mr Cauldwell, known to his friends as Spots. Spots is an accountant and because of his advice I have reconsidered my employment prospects.'

Spots stood up. He said to Warby, 'Where is it?'
'What?'
Spots jerked him up by his collar. 'You know what.'
Eddie put a hand on his associate. 'Leave him.'

130

Spots let go of Warby. 'I can't take this monkeying. Let's get it and go.'

You'd have to be pretty slow not to have caught up by then. We all knew what was wanted.

Eddie sighed, 'Sorry kids but I always listen to my accountant.'

Spots was looking around the racks. 'Where is it?'

The suitcase was further up the train, where we had been sitting before.

Spots swung a lumpy finger. 'We seen you with it. So what you done with it?'

I watched the tomatoes on his T-shirt. I could see his finger breaking their skin and juice spurting. Dad looked uncomfortable, he wasn't making the running, but neither was he arguing back. And Eddie, that creep, was still smiling and would carry on smiling while Spots cut our throats.

The carriage was practically empty. From where I sat I couldn't see anyone. If they could hear or see us Spots wasn't the sort of person they were likely to interrupt.

'We're not as daft as we look,' said Kathy with a short laugh that had too much cheek in it. 'We made our own plans.'

Spots turned to Dad. 'That girl has been badly brought up. She lacks parental control . . . '

Kathy came back, 'You want the money? Then you do some listening for a change.' Whatever I've said about my sister she is brave, or is it stupid? None of them answered her. Spots watched her like a cat a mouse. If she moved he'd go for her.

'I want to talk to you alone,' she said.

What was she up to?

'You kids clear off. I got something private to say.'

Warby said, 'You promised. You swore on your mother's grave . . . '

Kathy looked down at him as if he were in chains at her feet. She said to the men, 'You wanna hear what I gotta say – get rid of these kids.'

Eddie indicated with his head down the carriage. 'Go for a walk the three of you.'

We got up. Warby glowered at her. 'You do and I'll pack you in a can o' cat meat.'

She sniffed. 'Go for a walk, son. I got things to say to these gentlemen.'

Eddie laughed and Spots shoved us down the aisle.

I knew Kathy was stalling and Warby had been playing up to her. She could easily just have said where the suitcase was but she hadn't. She was allowing us to go to it.

And we did. We went back to our old seats. Above us was the suitcase. We all three looked at each other. Warby put a finger to his lips, stood up and looked about. Then quickly picked up the suitcase and brought it down to floor level. He sat back quietly and indicated for us to do the same.

We waited. No one running, no threats. They hadn't seen us. Warby got up and went to the carriage window and eased it down. He looked back at Kathy and the three men; she was obviously holding them with her tale. Warby picked up the suitcase and pushed it out the window.

It flew back. I put my head out. It jumped along the

gravel as if trying to get back on the train. Then gave up as the train rushed away, and lay dead beside the track.

Smaller and smaller. A quiet brown lump not even like a suitcase now. Too small, too far back to be a thing that could matter to anyone.

I turned back to the others. Warby was smiling.

'When we come to the station we go back for it.'

'Who?' said Sue.

'You two.'

24

Just as the train started I opened the door and jumped onto the platform. I turned round for Sue but she was being held back by Dad. He pulled her out of the way and stood in the doorway as the train picked up speed.

I don't know what went through his head. Did he know I was going to get the money? Maybe Kathy had run out of ideas. Maybe he just guessed. Maybe he didn't trust the others. Maybe it upset him that it was me running off. If it'd been Warby, or Sue or even Kathy he wouldn't have given a fig. I can't give his reasons – but I knew he wanted me back on the train.

I watched him. It was like a still photo. Him there in the door. Although the train was moving it didn't seem to be. It was too slow to matter. The click, click, clicks in my head just froze him at the door and froze the train. It seemed he would always be wondering whether to jump or not.

He jumped. There he was perhaps thirty yards up the platform, between me and the way out. He began to run towards me.

I was scared. I stepped onto a platform seat and dived

over the wooden fence without knowing what was behind it. There was a six-foot drop onto gravel.

I landed on my hands. They were bruised but the least of my troubles. I got back onto my feet and began to run.

I was on a country road, one side railway, the other hedgerow. Behind me I heard a thump. I turned. Dad was over, getting up and running after me.

I knew too that he'd catch me. I'd run off from Dad once and he'd hared after me, caught me before I'd gone fifty yards and tanned me there and then.

A car came round a bend, the driver hooted at me. I was running in the middle of the road. It sped past, the driver yelling at me. I glanced back – there was Dad too in the centre of the road coming at me, rocking and rolling.

'You come back here,' he called. 'When I catch you . . . '

He shook a fist. That for certain wasn't going to make me come back. I saw then he was limping, dragging his right foot. I guessed he must have hurt it when he came over the fence.

I concentrated on the running. If he was hurt I could get away. I needed to put enough distance between us then sneak off the road.

My throat was hurting and I had a stitch in my side. The hedge beside me was thick and thorny, over it I could see trees with small green apples. I pushed on round a bend where the hedge stopped and there was a wooden fence with open meadow and cows. Ahead another bend.

As I passed the cows looked up at me. A black and white one near the fence bellowed as I went past. Telling me to get back to my Dad.

On the bend was a side road. I took it. It was just a mud track with the ruts from a tractor on either side and a strip of grass and weeds in the middle. I ran along the middle, my breath sandpapering my throat. I glanced about. There was no one behind, but the flattened trail I was pushing through the weeds would make me a cinch to follow. I stepped into the tractor ruts, and stumbled along its bumps. Tiredness and the bumps rocked me each time I placed a foot. I stumbled, got up, went on; the only sound now my heavy breath.

A gate ahead. I hesitated. Should I? No one behind. Before I'd worked it all out I was climbing over and found myself in a field of cabbages. I stopped running and began to walk along its edge, sticking close to the hedge.

I didn't know whether Dad had even turned down the side road. If he was still going up the main road then I was safe here. But if he had taken the side road . . . He would be so angry. A sound of a twig cracking startled me. Across the cabbages I could see nothing. I ducked into the large leaves and waited.

The soil was hard and dry, the leaves thick as elephant's ears curling round centres of little cabbages. A spider fell onto me and scurried down my leg. Did it know the risk it was running? Maybe it did. Maybe it was running from its dad who wanted to eat it. It scampered along the soil and disappeared. I wished it luck.

I cautiously rose and went on. There was a rusty iron gate at the far corner of the field. I climbed over and walked along a rutted path in a grassy meadow, with flies buzzing around dried cow pats. Across the field were a few trees. I made for them.

They were oak trees with new acorns green in their cups. About the only tree I know. The trees were mossy and the ground underneath dried mud pitted with cows' hooves. I sat down behind a double oak that divided about two feet off the ground. Through the V I watched the entrance to the field.

I didn't know how long to wait. How long was safe. Or even how long was long. I thought about the train and wondered what was going on. Kathy, Warby and Sue with Eddie and Spots who wouldn't take kindly to no money and me jumping out. They were probably all in Leeds by now.

Except me and Dad.

The sound of a train in the distance brought me back to the suitcase lying by the track. I began to make my way back the way I had come with great care. Every few paces I stopped and listened. At the iron gate I watched the field of cabbages for several minutes before coming out and making my way back round the field.

I ran quickly up to the main road. There was nobody in either direction. Across the road was a wood behind a barbed wire fence. Somewhere beyond that was the railway track.

I lifted the rusted wire and carefully climbed through. The wood was thick with spindly saplings without any path. I just went the way I could, squeezing through, pushing young trees aside, climbing under. I scratched myself repeatedly on thorny wood and springy young branches.

I had never been in a wood like this before, with everything growing everywhere. Most of the ones I'd been in were looked after, parks really. But this was like jungle. I'd heard the word thicket and this must've been one.

I made my way where I could. Sometimes getting stuck and having to back out. Taking minutes to squeeze through hardly any ground at all. It made sense why it used to take them three years to cross Africa or Canada.

After a while I had lost my sense of direction. Was I still heading for the train line? A little way ahead was a taller tree. I fought my way to it and began to climb it. Once into the tree all I could see were leaves. I climbed higher, feeling shaky standing on the thin branches. Some way ahead the trees seemed to stop. Perhaps the track was there.

The sun was showing as a glow behind grey cloud. I took a direction from it and headed on.

It must've been about half an hour later I looked down on the track. I was scraped and miserable. But there was the suitcase only a few hundred yards away. I tried making my way along the fence but the trees were too thick against it. I climbed over, down the slope and ran along the track.

I picked up the case and made my way back over the fence and into the wood. If it was hard coming it was

138

worse going back humping the case. I only had one free hand and the extra weight made it doubly difficult.

That suitcase! Dragging it after me, pushing it in front of me. Spaces I could squeeze through it wouldn't go. Backing up. This way, that way. It felt like I was crossing Canada.

I made it. Scratched, bruised, hot and dirty.

Now on the road I realized the only good thing about the thicket. I couldn't be seen. Here on the road I was obvious.

I wanted to be far away. So there was no chance I could walk into Dad. But which way was far away – from Dad that is? Warby had said get to Leeds station. I just wanted to go back home. To be away from this mad chase. I guessed the circus had just been Eddie's tale so what was the point of going to Leeds?

My friends were there. The only people I knew. And I was stuck with the money. Lumbered with all this useless paper. Clever of Warby to suggest me and Sue go back. Getting himself out of it. You can't always tell how crafty Warby is being.

I trudged along. I heard a motor behind me. I turned and there was a single decker green bus. Country buses I remembered don't just stop at bus stops. I put my case down and waved.

It worked. The bus stopped a little ahead of me. I ran up to it.

It was a pay as you enter. The driver was a white-haired man with a swollen nose.

'Hop on.'

I did.

'Where do you want to go?'

I wanted to go anywhere. I couldn't say where.

'Come on, son, I ain't got all day.'

'Where you going?'

The place he said I didn't catch.

'Yes,' I said and fished out my money. All I had was my £5 note. The driver sighed heavily and sorted through his change. He gave me a ticket and I sat down.

There were only five people on the bus. Three women obviously together chatting away, a man in overalls and very grubby, and a young man in a baggy suit. I wondered where they were going. I wondered where I was going. It didn't matter much – all that mattered was leaving that place. I was getting away. I would sort out destinations later.

The bus pulled up at a stop. The doors opened and my dad got on.

25

'Hello, Davey.' Like we always met on this bus.

'Hello, Dad.' A voice out of my shoes. He sat next to me and took the suitcase. I was shut in against the window.

'You led me a chase,' he said wearily. I wondered where he had been the last few hours.

Then he seemed to forget me. He leaned forward with his arms on the seat in front so I couldn't see his face very well. His hair looked even thinner from the side and was going grey round the ears. The collar of his lumberjacket was curling and the jacket itself scruffy. He needed a shave.

I wanted to see his face. To make out what he was thinking. But all I could see was cheek, a bit of tight mouth, a near-closed eye. Although I couldn't see him well I didn't like his mood. Whatever it was – it wasn't friendly.

The bus seemed to be going everywhere, round in circles. I was sure we'd been on this bit of road before. A crowd of schoolgirls got on. All in school uniform, carrying bags and hockey sticks. The bus was packed out with their red and white check dresses and funny straw hats.

At any other time I would have found their noise a nuisance; shouting across each other, laughing and giggling, twenty conversations at once – but now I found it safe. Dad couldn't do anything as long as they were here.

He couldn't lean forward on the seatback because of the girls in front. He slouched, rocking in his seat, biting a finger and breathing heavily. The chatter of the girls was annoying him. That worried me.

He turned to me and said, 'I've got a screaming headache.' I saw it stretched across his eyes.

He couldn't stop moving in his seat. Backwards and forwards, rubbing his forehead with his fingers, his hands, his forearm. I had the feeling that any minute he was going to blow.

We were coming into a town. The girls began to filter off. Dad suddenly got up, took the suitcase, took my arm as if I were an extra piece of luggage, and we got off.

The day was cooler than it had been earlier and it looked as if it might rain. We walked past small houses, their doors on the street, then along a narrow pavement by a row of shops. There were quite a few people about and the main road was busy with traffic.

We came to a chemist and Dad led me in. He went to the drugs counter. From his inside pocket he drew out a number of scraps of paper. With the suitcase between his legs he searched them through, opening them out. One of them was a prescription. It was dirty and dog-eared.

A young woman in a white coat was behind the counter. He gave her the prescription. She shook her head.

'I'm afraid that's out of date.'

'I need it,' said Dad.

She shook her head again, lips pursed. 'Sorry.'

Dad leaned forward. 'My head's killing me.'

She picked up a flat tin from the counter. 'Have you tried these?'

Angrily he tore them from her. 'These are no good!'

The woman looked frightened. The other customers in the shop were watching.

'I'm sorry, sir,' she said quietly.

He turned round to the shop and held up the tin. 'My head's killing me and all she can offer is these sweets.'

'It's out of date,' she said, leaning back against the cupboard behind her, to be out of his reach.

'Is my bloody head out of date!'

He threw the box onto the floor and crunched it under his foot. 'Useless, useless,' he moaned.

He picked up the case and my arm and we rushed through the shop.

A little way further we sat on a church wall. Dad's limp was getting worse. Behind us a bumpy graveyard, the grass parched like straw. One grave nearby had fresh flowers in a little vase. I strained across to look. It said 1943, beloved son. It brought tears to my eyes.

Someone coming every week and putting out flowers all these years.

Dad was turning the prescription round and round, scraping one ankle against the other and grimacing.

'It's all your fault,' he growled. 'You're nothing but a flaming nuisance.'

There was no answer to that.

'Take it,' he pushed the prescription in my hand.

It was hardly readable, covered in dirty fingermarks.

'Change it,' he said, and gritted through his teeth as some pain went through him as he handed me a pen.

I looked at it.

'The date, the date,' he said feverishly.

I looked at him. I looked at it. To what?

'Change the three to a seven.'

It was a very curly three indicating the third month. There were no straight lines in it. How could I alter it to a seven?

'Change it,' he yelled.

I put it on the wall and the pen poked through the paper. 'I need something to rest on.'

Dad brought up the suitcase and put it on the wall. I knew I couldn't do it but I thought he would belt me if I didn't. I used the top of the three as the top of the seven and drew a line through the curly back of the three. Now it looked like neither.

Dad took it. 'What do you call that? Is that what they teach you at school?'

Not to forge prescriptions I thought.

He rubbed it with his grubby fingers and made it

even dirtier. He wet his fingers and rubbed some more. The paper began to rub away.

He looked up at me. 'It's all your fault.'

He screwed up the prescription and threw it into the churchyard. Then he got up, pulled me roughly and we walked down the main road of the town.

He was limping badly now, walking on the toe of his injured leg, unable to put his heel down. After a short while he stopped, leaned against a shop window and stood on one leg.

'I gotta rest up, Davey.'

The sound of my name surprised me. Like I was a friend now and not a flaming nuisance.

'Over there, Davey.' My name again.

We crossed the road. He stopped me outside a red-brick building. It said Heathcliff Hotel, AA listed. There was a porch on the street and a glass door. Dad tried it. It opened. Dad ushered me in front, into a small carpeted room. A few low soft chairs and a coffee table with an ashtray in the form of a black boot. At one end was a counter.

Dad pressed the buzzer.

26

Dad lay on the bed snoring, a forearm over his eyes.

I was on the floor. From there I couldn't see Dad but I could hear his squeezebox breathing. Earlier I had turned the TV on, with the sound down low. Dad had bellowed out, 'Put that bloody thing off.'

Above me I could hear the babble of a set, like voices talking through water. From time to time a door closed somewhere, the plumbing vibrated.

There were two single beds in the room, side by side, each with a peach bedspread. There was hardly any room between the beds, I could just get through walking sideways. By the side of each bed was a wooden chair, painted white and stained.

The room didn't look real. I tried to think what it reminded me of. Then it came to me. Auntie Alice had some pictures of her doll's house. Close-ups, so that you might think the rooms were real but you could see they weren't. This room was like that. Empty, too tidy, nothing personal. Things placed to look like a real room but the two armchairs, the sideboard, even the TV on its single leg were like not very good models. It was a cheap doll's house and whoever owned it didn't play with it much.

The room had a strange sweet smell; staleish, now mixed with Dad's socks. I tried to open a window but it was jammed. With the door locked nothing could get out or in.

A fly was buzzing, making barbed wire patterns in the air. It seemed to have no idea where it wanted to go.

Like this trip. I didn't know where we were. Not too far from Leeds was the best I could say. Where we were going next I had as much idea as that fly.

It landed on Dad's face. I watched it crawling over his nose, then down his cheek as if he were dead. It walked into his open mouth, shuffling in the stickiness on his tongue. I thought he'll choke as I looked fascinated at his fillings and the skim of liquid in the back of the mouth. He breathed the fly out and it flew off to the window, bashing against the glass. It couldn't get out either.

I wondered if I could get the key out of his pocket. Except I didn't know which pocket it was in.

I thought of murder. A dopey idea. Apart from the fact there was nothing to do it with – anyone would know it was me. That didn't stop me thinking about it.

I pressed my thumbs together and opened out my hands. With gritted teeth I made slowly for him, intent on his neck. I came down on it – as close as I could without touching.

I didn't want to touch him.

I had seen a dead body once; in a coffin. My

grandmother was laid out in her sitting room in her best clothes. They tried to make her look asleep but no one sleeps so stiffly, their arms crossed like that. Mum had kissed her and I didn't know how she could do that.

Like my dad now. I couldn't touch him.

A wave of loneliness hit me. As long as I could remember I seemed to be on my own. Just when we got friends we would move on.

Why didn't people like me?

I was short and I was only good at maths. What a useless thing to be good at! People just had a go at you for it. Not like football or karate or some real talent.

I had to have that money. With money you'd always have friends. There'd be plenty around to play with, to listen. They'd want what I'd got.

Take my mum and dad. They must've had some chances and they missed the lot. Look at him catching flies. And Mum in a dump flat. She hates him and he wants her back. How crackers! She works like a slave and never has a penny, and heaven only knows what Dad does but he drinks it when he gets it.

I didn't want to be like them in twenty years.

A suitcase full of my money. I could cry now. How I wanted it. How I needed it.

Once in school a sparrow came into our classroom through the window. We tried to catch it to let it out. It went crashing against the walls, flying wildly, smashing from wall to wall. If we hadn't opened every window it would have killed itself.

I was like that sparrow except I wouldn't crash against the walls. I wanted to alright. To tell everyone what I felt, to scream it all out. But I wouldn't. How I wanted to. But I wouldn't.

Dad stretched, let out a noisy yawn, and sat up.

'That's better.' He rubbed his eyes. 'I needed that.'

He got out of bed and immediately collapsed on his ankle. Sitting on the floor, making short noises of pain, he drew back his sock. The ankle was swollen, puffed out like a white sausage.

He shook his head. 'That's fun that is.' And gave a soft chuckle. 'Not exactly set up for a quick getaway am I?'

Dad filled the sink with hot water, stood on a chair and bathed the injured ankle, letting out gasps of pain as he massaged the swelling. Balanced dangerously, I thought if he slips he won't even be hopping.

He hobbled over to the bed and lay back, the ankle red and steaming, a relaxed grin on his face. He seemed proud of his ankle.

'Whatdja think of that? Eh?'

'Could be broken,' I said.

He chuckled. 'Cheerful. That's what I like about you. Cheerful.'

He took a pillow from behind him and removed the case. He folded the pillow case in half longwise and began to put it round his ankle. First he just rolled it round but that slipped up his leg. Then he put it under his foot and then round his ankle pulling it as tight as he could and tucking the loose end in. Dad swung over to the edge of the bed, picked up a sock and put it over the makeshift bandage.

It was funny with that sweaty sock at the end. Like a sticky bud about to burst into some strange flower.

'What you grinning at?'

I couldn't help it. It looked so funny.

'Your good looks.' Then I started laughing and Dad looking at me started laughing. I walked around the room giggling away. I tried to stop myself, turned back and saw Dad and began again.

Dad was laughing so much tears were running down his face. That was amazing to see, my dad laughing, then it suddenly occurred to me maybe he was thinking the same.

We both stopped and looked at each other grinning.

'Davey,' he said, 'come here.'

I came and sat by him on the bed.

He ruffled my hair. His face softer, all gone the murder and hate I had run from.

'Tell me, Dad,' I said. 'Why didn't you get the eleven o'clock train?'

'Eh?'

'At King's Cross. Why were you on the same train as me and Warby?'

He laughed, his eyes creasing in the corners. 'Cuz we saw you, Davey. Stuffing yourselves in the cafe. We saw you miss the eleven o'clock, and we saw the one you got on.'

I should've guessed. But I had a few more questions, and since he was answering . . .

'There's no circus is there, Dad?'

'Afraid not, Davey.'

'So why did you send us to Leeds? I mean . . . why not Southend?'

Dad slapped his lips, and made thinking noises. Finally he spoke looking down at his nails, 'We could've just done a snatch. Grabbed the suitcase off you – but we might've been seen. Anyway I didn't want violence. Neither did Eddie . . . So I was to distract the two of you – while Spots did the business. I had a few options; one was to treat you to a meal in the buffet car. That had to be a long distance train.'

'Didn't have to be Leeds though.'

He gave a short laugh. 'We had it all worked out.' He ruffled my hair. 'Get the money, then train from Doncaster to Hull, and boat to Rotterdam . . . What a load of smarties!' He stopped in a wince, and rubbed his ankle.

'Where did you meet them?'

He looked me over pursing his lips. 'You should've been a copper.'

'Where?'

'Parkhurst. Shared a cell. A couple of weeks ago we got together on a business venture . . . and this came up.'

'What business?'

'Enough, Davey.' His voice a little sharper. 'You're a good kid, but ease up on the questions.'

'Sorry, Dad.'

'S'alright, Davey. Just don't push me.'

I didn't want him in a bad mood again. To make some space I walked to the window and looked down at the traffic. The sun was setting and the streetlights had come on, though it wasn't dark yet.

I turned to him, 'Am I still your prisoner?'

He put his hand in his trouser pocket and took out a key. I walked across and he put the key in my hand, squeezing it as he did so. I went to the door and unlocked it. Then threw him back the key.

'Davey,' he said quietly. 'How'd you like to go to Brazil?'

The question caught me from nowhere. It was not the sort of thing you had an answer for. I just didn't know what to say. He might as well have said Mars.

'We got a lot of money here,' he said.

I was beginning to understand what he was saying. It overpowered me.

'They don't know where we are,' he said. 'We could go anywhere.'

I said weakly, 'Not with a suitcase full of money.'

He had his injured leg out and was slowly revolving his foot.

'I know someone in Amsterdam. They'll buy the money off us.'

'Buy the money?'

He laughed. 'It's no good in a suitcase is it. He'll buy it for 75 per cent of the value and give us a cheque. Then we open a bank account in an international bank.'

Dad suddenly reached into his pocket and brought out a jackknife. He reached down for the suitcase and stabbed the knife in. He drew the knife along until he had a flap of plastic. He folded it back until we could just see the bank notes.

'Just making sure I didn't have a second lot of under-wear.' He laughed.

'Why Brazil?' I said.

He sucked in air like he'd eaten something hot. 'Cuz they won't like it, Davey. Spots and Eddie are expecting their share of this – and if we're going to cut them out we've got to go a long way.'

Brazil? I'd drawn this picture of South America for geography. Warby had put eyes and a mouth on it so it was like a dog's head. Brazil was the nose. Rubber, Coffee, Carnival. Didn't they speak Portuguese?

'You hungry?' asked Dad.

I nodded.

'Let's get some grub and talk it out.'

27

I quietly rose. Slipped into my clothes as swiftly as I dared without making a sound. It was light enough by the streetlamps. After the restaurant Dad had left me to watch TV and had gone down to the bar. When he came back I was in bed. He kept calling me but I pretended to be asleep.

If I had been asleep he would certainly have woken me, the noise he made undressing, falling about, talking to himself. He kept stopping to stroke my head. I had to lay dead as he told me how great it was going to be in Brazil.

I looked at him. Asleep on the bed, fully clothed, mouth opening as he snorted at each breath. My dad. Nothing was going to wake him.

I picked up the case and opened the door. Closing it behind me I tiptoed along the hallway lit by a single light. Down the stairs.

The hotel was eerily quiet; almost as if it were empty. Or haunted. I was trembling at the thought of meeting someone. Even if they were human – what would I say to them?

The foyer stank with cigar smoke but was cleaned of

any other signs of life. The ashtrays were empty, the chairs straight – they seemed to be looking at me, waiting for me.

I made my way to the front door.

It was locked.

In panic I swung the handle, pulled the bolts – even though I could see the lock was on.

I stood in the half light, looking into the empty street through the glass door. It was raining, the road surface gleaming from the streetlamps. The rain looked so cool, so refreshing as it pipped into the puddles, coming through the lamplight like bright pins.

A shout from afar moved me. I crept back to bed.

Dad woke me in the morning with a cup of tea. It wasn't until I started to drink that I wondered how he got it. He must've hopped down the stairs to reception, then hopped up again.

He was sitting on the side of my bed adjusting his makeshift bandage. He didn't have tea himself. I thought what a lot of trouble he went to.

He said, 'How d'you fancy the seaside?'

I didn't know what I fancied but I said, 'Sounds alright.'

'Scoff that and let's go.'

We sat in the foyer while the receptionist phoned a cab for us. Through the glass door I could see the day was bright and sunny.

Dad sat in an armchair leaning forward, having a smoke.

'A good day for the sea,' he said.

I was looking out into the street. The shadow of

a lamppost stretched along the pavement. A woman opposite was pulling down a red and white sun shade with a wooden pole.

'Davey?'

I turned to him. He tapped the seat beside him. 'Come here.'

I sat down.

He said, 'I gotta rest up for a couple of days. This ankle. Then we'll be off?'

Brazil?

'The two of us we can make a good team. We got what we need now, we stick together. We don't have to think about anyone else.'

I'd been thinking about Mum. She'd be worrying now when we didn't come home from school yesterday. I hoped Kathy had phoned Mrs Chester, our neighbour.

I said, 'Can I phone Mum?'

His face screwed. 'Safer if you don't.'

Safer for who?

He squeezed my hand. 'It'll all be different now. Soon as we get away from everything. Me and you.' He clicked his tongue and sighed. 'You may not think I cared what with your mum and all but I did alright. I used to think about you all the time. How you were growing up. How you wouldn't know me. How you'd never really had a chance to know me.'

Gripping my shoulder he said, 'You've always been important to me, Davey.'

He looked away.

'Lots of things I done I ain't been proud of. I been

wild. I know I get angry sometimes but that don't mean I can't love. That don't mean I don't need love.'

After a pause he said, 'I wish your mother knew that.'

A black man in shorts and T-shirt stood in the door. 'Cab?'

We went out onto the street.

The cabbie was young and muscular. I thought he must do weights.

I got in the back seat. Dad handed me the suitcase. It was hot in the car.

Outside Dad was talking to the driver who was frowning and shaking his head. I could see Dad getting heated. The driver just shook his head. Dad put his hand in his pocket and got out some notes. He put them in the man's hand. The man looked at them in amazement. Then he nodded.

They both got in and we set off. Dad sat next to the driver which meant I could stretch out in the back.

After a minute we stopped. Dad hobbled out and went into a sports shop.

The driver was looking at me through his mirror.

He said, 'He's got a lot of money.'

I didn't reply.

He said, 'Is he a gambling man?'

'Yes,' I said.

The cabbie slapped the wheel and laughed. 'Tomorrow he'll lose it all.'

Dad came out of the shop with a blue suitcase with wheels on the bottom. He got back in and the cabbie stowed it in the boot.

Quite soon we had left the town. The countryside was hilly and the car really motoring. I imagined rounding a bend and hitting a tree. The car then rolling over and down the side of the hill, me and the suitcase thrown out and Dad and the driver rolling on.

There they lay far below in a heap of twisted metal. I picked up the suitcase and climbed back up to the road.

Then I'd go to Amsterdam and sell the money to a man who'd set me up with an international bank account.

I'd have to change my clothes. It's no good looking like a schoolkid and spending big money. You have to look the part. Smart clothes, expensive shoes. A good hairstyle. Rings and a posh watch.

Then it wouldn't matter I was a kid. 'Cept I didn't talk right. Rich kids went to posh schools and talked la-di-da. Pop stars had money though and a lot of them talked normal.

I practised saying 'first class to Los Angeles please' and 'a room overlooking the sea'. I would be a mystery. Rich, smart, jet setting and they would all want to know who I was. I would tell them my mum and dad died in a plane crash.

No. Then they would think I wasn't really rich but just living off the insurance. I would say my father got ten years for spying in Russia and my mother committed suicide. . . . No. I didn't want my mother committing suicide. A mental hospital – no, nor that either. She had divorced my father, remarried and gone to live in Brazil.

Dad was snoozing in the front seat. The driver had put on sunglasses, the type that looked like mirrors. I could see him in the driving mirror but I couldn't tell whether he was looking at me or not.

Suppose I bought an island in the South Seas? Who would I invite to live with me? Warby? Maybe I would but only if he apologized. Mum could come but just on visits. How would I tell her that? That I didn't want her all the time.

What if Kathy came? She'd bring Sue and I couldn't stop them unless I had a private army and that would just be a waste of money. Feeding them and housing them, and them marching everywhere and half the island for their shooting range.

Forget the island.

We were climbing a steep hill. The car was whining as we came out through the trees into fields at the top. Suddenly I saw the sea.

28

I followed Dad to the change kiosk. The cashier was a young man with cropped black hair and a long scar down his left cheek that made me think they'd been robbed.

He pushed us the bags of tens with hands that were blistered, the fingernails bitten back to the quick and black with grease. Maybe he'd spent the morning working under a fairground machine. Dad gave me one of the bags.

I'm not that good at arcade machines. Now Warby he's an ace. Half the machines I can't understand. Like you can jump into hyperspace when you push the button but it only works when something else is happening. Warby takes all that in his stride. With one hand he's shooting away and with the other avoiding all the shots coming at him, while with me I can only seem to do one at a time. Either I'm shooting like crazy and space invaders are coming at me from all angles and Poof! – I'm dead, or I'm running this way and that and shooting nothing so they're all coming and coming. I enjoy watching Warby. Although I like playing myself I don't like it so much as watching a good player. The speed, the reflexes, their excitement – I pick up on their excitement.

It seemed Dad was the same way. He didn't want to spend any. Just watch me spend it. Twenty quid in 10p pieces!

I had half a dozen goes on the space invaders. Then I went on one of those racing games when you drive a car along and cars keep coming for you. It's amazing how exciting that is. You feel like you're moving when of course you're not. Half a dozen goes at that was enough though.

Then pinball. Well that's alright but four goes and I had my wack. I pushed some money in the fruit machines. I even had four going at once like I saw in this film about Las Vegas. You have to see how many you can fill before the first one stops.

Suddenly I'd had enough. I have never been in this situation before. Always in an arcade I've run out of money. Like I've had a quid or something; a few goes at 10p a few at 20p and that's it. Now I'd spent 10 quid and I was bored.

Dad pushed me on. Try that one, that one or that one. I was getting bored silly.

In the end I sat down at the bingo just for a break. I can't stand bingo, specially at seasides. The callers have those dead-flat voices, like they're talking in their sleep. Like I suppose anyone would who'd been doing it all day for the past three months.

I took two boards. There was only six of us playing. Dad stood over my shoulder. The caller was pretty speedy. None of that messing about with two little ducks, twenty-two. It was 'on the yellow number one' then with hardly a pause 'on the blue number ten'. I could hardly keep up, Dad was pointing them out to me. Suddenly Dad shouted 'Bingo' – like I'd won the football pools or something.

I ended up with a stuffed horse.

Dad suggested some lunch.

We had a good feed-up. It wasn't just one of your greasy seaside cafes but a restaurant. They had a wine list and a proper menu. The waiters in suits embarrassed me. They're so polite they make me want to puke. All round you with the menu and it's all got fancy names. I thought give me self-service anytime.

Dad wasn't any happier. He had a scared look, like a sheep that's accidentally walked into a butchers. In the end he asked them what they recommended and he said he'd have it.

Having got the ordering done with it was great after that. From melon to ice-cream gateau with soup and a main course in between. We finished with coffee and cheese board.

Afterwards we sat on the promenade in a couple of deckchairs bloated. The sun was beautiful and I felt like a king. Relaxed, warm, well fed. I lay back in the chair and closed my eyes, my lids like a bright velvet curtain. Around me the sounds of the beach and prom. This was bliss.

I snoozed off for maybe half an hour. Could've been longer. Who was counting?

'Fancy a swim?' asked Dad.

Why not? Dad hopped across the road and a few

minutes later came back with a couple of swimming costumes and beach towels. We went down on the beach, took over a couple of vacant deckchairs, wrapped ourselves in our towels, wriggled out of our clothes and into our costumes.

Both of us were horribly white. Like plants from under a stone.

Dad said, 'Enjoying yourself?'

'Yeh.' And it was true I was. I was shoving the real world to the back of my head. This was all there was. This little world on the beach. No other people in other places worrying or hunting for us.

Dad said, 'No way will they find us here.'

How could they? I didn't even know where we were.

'We can do this every day in Rio.' He beamed. 'Life's not so bad with your old dad.'

'Yeh.' Maybe it would be alright in Brazil. Out of the flats. No school. Lying on the beach. Big meals. Clear nights. The Milky Way along the sky like a silver ribbon round a parcel. With a telescope I could draw the stars in so close, it would be like I was in space.

'We'll buy a house. Start you off with a private tutor so you pick up the lingo then you can go to school.'

Oh.

He was laid back, his eyes closed, and a smile of perfect contentment.

'Half the money we'll invest in some business. Maybe a hotel.'

Two children in front of us were digging a large hole. They were both standing in it and furiously throwing up the sand. I thought busy little sods; like the whole human race, digging sand pits for the sea to fill in again. But not us. In Brazil we'd throw in our spades.

Their parents were lying a little way off on inflatable mattresses. The man was really hairy with a large beer gut. I thought – wonder what they'd do with quarter of a million. I grinned as I imagined going up to them and saying, 'Here's 10,000. It's yours if you can answer these three skill-testing questions.' The first two'd be really easy to wind 'em up but the third'd be a real toughy.

'Let's swim,' said Dad.

We made our way down to the water. The sand changed to pebbles. We walked carefully on tiptoes, putting one foot down before picking up the other.

Then sand again and then the cold surf. We walked ankle deep. Oh it was cold. Dad splashed me. I leaped away. We walked in further. As the waves came I jumped to keep the water off my upper half.

Dad dived. He swam a few strokes and then surfaced.

I walked out further shivering. My arms high above me. I winced as my costume became covered. And then I swam.

At least I was cold all over. There was nothing more for the sea to get at.

We swam along the beach. Both swimming breaststroke. Swimming easy. It was a cold paradise. And over on my back to a blue sky and the sounds of the beach. Warm and cold at once.

We stopped swimming. The sea was up to my neck

164

and came halfway up Dad's chest. His hair lay over his forehead like seaweed on a rock.

'Great eh?'

'Smashing.'

He shook his wet hair and looked up to the sky. 'What a life!' he called and leapt out of the water.

I dived into the green. Like looking through a marble. Cheeks bulging, pulling through the thick water to the cloudy bottom, and then pushing up and bursting out into the sky.

Dad was heading towards the beach. He turned and called to me, 'Won't be a minute. I'm just going to buy a dingy.'

I watched him stretch out of the water and hobble up the beach, his back slightly bent and his arms dangling. Thin and white.

I lay on my back and swam away from the beach.

In Brazil the sky would be always blue like this. I would be free, Dad would be free. It would be like being born again. Change, a chance to be different. To go to the front of the queue instead of always being at the back.

What of Mum? I don't know. And Warby? There would be losses. More than I could make up?

I turned over and swam out. Too much thinking too quick. Let it run over like the green water. All that thinking would just think it away. Let me swim through and take what came. Like those sailing boats and the floating buoys.

Everything was OK. I was here and swimming and the world had everything to offer me. And I was ready to take it. I wasn't just another mouse on a dump. It was my world. I didn't have to dream I was better or bigger, or living somewhere else. Because I was better and bigger and living somewhere else.

I could cope with Dad. He loved me and I could get over the bad parts. I wasn't a kid.

So much water, so much beautiful water. And so much sky. There's hardly any in the city. It comes in cut-up strips. But it's a dome! I never knew that before. Like a huge cake dish with me right in the middle. It moves along with you. I'm always in the middle.

I turned and it turned. There's the people on the beach. Waiting. I was tired, beautifully tired. Like part of the sea.

On my back and easy. Like the first amphibian about to crawl up the beach, ready for a new life.

I touched bottom and stood. I was a little along the beach, the water up to my chest. I searched for Dad among the deckchairs.

There he was.

Standing over him was Spots. Just further up the beach coming in on them was Eddie with the two girls and Warby.

29

They were waving their arms and pushing. I could hear their shrill voices from where I crouched behind the breakwater. I couldn't see Dad. Spots and Eddie stood over the deckchair where he must've been sitting.

The whole beach was looking at them. Then Spots and Eddie sat down on the sand. Their voices died. They were obviously going for a cooler approach.

Just beyond them, also sitting, were Warby, Kathy and Sue. Warby was digging a hole. Kathy and Sue were playing with pebbles. Why hadn't they got away?

I began to make my way up the breakwater, crouching low. I wound my way through the deckchairs and sunbathing bodies. No one took much notice of me. They probably thought I was hiding from a kid.

Once on the promenade I ran. Across the road, through the crazy golf, up the stairs onto the cliff road. I tripped on the top step and fell.

I got up. My knee hurt and my hand was grazed. I massaged my knee and hoped it was nothing much. I walked on slowly, at first hobbling but then my stride returned. My hand was stinging but my knee felt just a bit bruised.

I broke into a run. The cliff road twisted back on itself. I could see the beach from where I had come. I saw what I didn't want to see. They were walking up the beach.

Ignoring pain I stretched up the hill. At the top the traffic lights were in my favour. I crossed over and up the steps of the Majestic Hotel.

I went to the reception.

'Keys for twenty-seven.'

I took them and bounded up the stairs. Once in the room I grabbed the suitcase, the one we'd bought with wheels. We'd junked the old one. At the door the craziness of it hit me. A large suitcase and no clothes. I'd left them on the beach!

I looked around the room. Dad had left a few crumpled £20 notes on the table. I picked them up, took the suitcase in my other hand and left.

Once in the lobby I attempted to walk coolly through. The receptionist called out, 'Are you checking out, sir?'

'Yes,' I said and dropped the keys and the notes on the counter.

As I headed for the swing doors the receptionist called, 'Your change, sir.'

'Keep it,' I said as I went through.

From the steps I could see them coming up the cliff road. I dived into the hotel shrubbery. Turned the suitcase on end behind a shrub and squatted down.

They came into the hotel drive. Dad was hobbling in front, Eddie was close by, and Spots was in the rear pushing Warby and the girls.

They stopped at the steps. Eddie and Spots had an

168

argument about who should and shouldn't go in. They might as well have had a microphone. Finally Eddie and Dad went up the steps, leaving Spots outside to guard the others.

Spots was in a huff. He was walking round and round wiping the sweat off his face with his hands, then wiping them on his dirty T-shirt. At the same time shouting at Warby and the girls who sat on the steps.

I waited until Spots had his back to me, then I rose a little and waved. Kathy saw me. She immediately whispered to the others.

Spots turned and I hid down. He lit himself a cigarette and looked up at the hotel. There couldn't be much time before they came out again.

Spots turned away. I tipped the suitcase and pointed to it. Warby who was looking at me nodded. They had a quick whisper and suddenly the three of them shot off in different directions.

'Oi, come back,' yelled Spots, undecided who to go for, finally deciding on Kathy.

I pulled out of the shrubbery and out of the hotel drive. I felt a push in the back. Warby was there.

I was so happy to be with him. We briefly clasped hands.

'Down the cliff road,' he yelled.

We crossed over, set the suitcase on its wheels, and one on either side whizzed it down the hill.

I hung onto the handle as the case ran away. Warby was running flat out smashing it with the flat of his hand.

An old man and woman were coming up the cliff

road. We hurtled towards them. There was no stopping us. They jumped into the road as we careered past.

The case was dragging me. Warby was beating it more and more. Suddenly my legs tied under me. I let go of the case and sprawled forward into the wall by the side of the road.

I lay flat out and looked up to see Warby running away with the case. Miraculously I didn't seem to be hurt. I got up and continued running.

Rounding the last bend I bumped pell mell into Warby flinging us both to the ground. He lay there grinning like he'd just won the Olympic marathon. Out of breath, scared, I would still have forgiven Warby anything for just being there.

We got up and crossed over to the promenade where we began to run again. This time Warby pulled and I pushed from behind.

We got up a fair lick. Nothing like as fast as on the hill though. That was crackers. We were tired now and there was no slope to help. Our slower speed made it easier for us to get round pedestrians or for them to get out of our way.

We passed a row of bathing huts. Then a row of deckchairs facing the sea. Then a shelter, full of old people, sitting there frowning as we came past. Past the pier, past boat rides and a row of kiosks. On the other side was a funfair and the arcade where I had played.

'Slow it, slow it,' I called to Warby.

'We gotta make some distance.'

My lungs were rasping, my legs heavy. I couldn't go on like this. No matter who was behind.

Then without warning Warby stopped and I practically hit him. I looked up. For the past minute my eyes had only been on the case. I sucked in air desperately.

'It's the end of the road,' Warby said breathlessly.

The road just stopped at the cliff face which jutted out. There were steps going up to the top, and half a dozen going down to the sand.

Warby said, 'On the beach.'

We jumped down to it.

There were handles on both ends of the case. Warby took the front and me the back. It was impossible to run carrying the case and the beach was pebbly. Warby was striding away like an East German walking champion. To hell with him I thought and let go of the case. Warby turned on me.

'It's alright for you,' I said, 'you got shoes.'

Warby took his shoes off and then his socks. He held his socks out.

'Have these.'

I put them on and we started off again. It was better but not a lot, especially with Warby striding away.

There were few people on this beach. It was away from the town and more pebbles than Brighton. Just as I was getting used to them we crossed a breakwater and the beach became rocky. Dark green slippery rock with pools between. Great if you were looking for crabs. Murder to clamber across with a suitcase.

We slipped and slid. With just one hand free I figured

one of us was going to crack their head open, especially at the pace Warby was still forcing.

Then we stopped and I reckoned it was because Warby needed a rest. He pointed out two starfish in a clear pool, between a lettuce sort of seaweed. Around the pool were purple anemones; like little shaving brushes.

Warby put his hand in and picked up a starfish. He handed it to me; it was rough like pumice.

I carefully put it back.

'How did they know me and Dad were here?'

'We got a taxi from the station and the driver told us about his mate who'd picked up a man and a kid. How the man had given him 100 quid to take him to the seaside.'

I remembered our driver's face when Dad gave him the notes.

'So they gave him 50 quid to find his mate,' said Warby.

'And he found him.'

'Yep.'

'A big black man?'

'Yep.'

'And he said we were here?'

'Yep.'

An anemone was huffing and puffing like a squashed cigar.

'Why didn't you run off?' I said.

He smiled. 'Why didn't you?'

He was standing in the pool in his shoes, the bottoms of his trousers wet.

'What we going to do?'

Warby shrugged.

'My Dad wants me to go to Brazil.'

Warby frowned.

'To start a new life.'

'Not when Eddie and Spots have done with him.'

'Look.' I pointed to two distant figures coming up the beach from where we'd just come. One very tall.

'Come on,' yelled Warby.

We picked up the case and headed over the rocks. If we had seen them they had probably seen us.

As we scrambled on I looked at the cliffs, searching for a way up. They were sheer. In places great lumps had fallen away and lay underneath.

We rounded a rock onto clear sand. I noticed for the first time how close the sea was.

'The tide's coming in.'

The sea was hardly thirty foot from the cliff edge.

I saw a flush of fear in Warby's face. He shook his head. 'We can't go back.'

We pushed on over the sand. Maybe up ahead round that next rock the land might be higher. Or there might be a way up the cliff.

We had begun to jog. A lump jog, heavy and puffy, the case bashing my knees and the back of Warby's legs. I looked behind; two longs rows of prints zig-zagging in the soft sand. In front Warby's back bumping up and down. Beside us the brown-streaked cliffs, near enough to touch.

Ahead of us the cliff jutted out into the sea. We paddled into the surf to go round it. Round the other side the sea had already reached the cliffs. But was only a few inches deep at the base where we splashed through.

In no time we were soaked. Hot from running, cold from the sea. As we jogged I pushed with my free arm against the cliff which was green alongside us. In panic I realized the high water mark was over our heads. This was crazy. I let go of the suitcase. It sloshed into the water. Warby brought to a halt, turned.

'We'll drown,' I yelled.

'Or be murdered,' he said.

He picked up the case in his two hands and looked at me. I shook my head. Warby turned away and dragged himself on.

'You're nuts, Warby.'

I watched him straining through the surf, wet hair clinging to the back of his neck. A sudden chill ran through me. Whatever we did was crazy.

I began running after Warby. I needed my friend. He was my only hope.

I caught him just at the round of the bay. I took hold of the back handle. He didn't look back and we jogged on.

We climbed over a jut of green rocks and slid down into the next bay. The sea reached to our knees. Frothy waves crashed off the cliffs splashing us all over.

Without Warby I would have sat down in the surf and waited. For the men. Or for the sea. Whichever came first. I was so tired all I could do was follow.

Warby turned to me. His face wet in misery and dog-tiredness.

'Next bay,' he gasped.

I nodded. Next bay paradise. Next bay Brazil.

When we reached it, to our dismay, the sea was still higher. On or back? We knew what was behind . . . We lifted the suitcase to our heads and pressed in close to the cliff as we entered the water which came to our waists.

A large wave hit us. I stumbled and kept my feet, Warby fell and the case came after.

I scrambled to him just as the next wave threw him down. This time he got up quicker. The case had been picked up by the retreating wave and was floating on its side barely above the surface. Warby waded out to it, rocking like a drunk. He bent down and struggled to lift it from the water.

'Come on,' he screamed at me.

I was thrown by a wave. With effort I got up and made my way to Warby who was dragging the case through the water. I took the back handle with both hands. We did not have the strength to lift it to our heads.

We moved on like lost links in a chain, our hands welded to the case. Pushing, pushing and hardly moving at all while the sea threw everything at us.

Ahead was a black rock, like a craggy whale beached on a reef. Its stub nose stretched skywards, and the sea, squeezed between cliff and rock, lashed at it in tongues of white water.

'Let me have a go,' shouted Warby.

He left me with the case. The sea threw itself at him as if it had been waiting. Somehow he kept to his feet and in a lull between waves made it to the rock. Where it came out from the cliff it was about his height with no footholds. He tried to press his fingers from the top but was too weak to get any lift. A fierce wave threw him against the cliff.

Warby staggered back to me. He took the case and made his way back. A wave hit him. And another. What held him up I don't know. He was drenched and shaking but still standing. He made it to the rock and flattened himself against it as a wave came. When it drew back he turned the case on end, stepped on it, and heaved himself up the rock.

I tried to follow. Perhaps I knew I couldn't. Perhaps I was just too tired. The first wave threw me down. I rose and was thrown again. I tried once more and was dragged flat into the surf. I could see nothing but water. Thrashing mad bubbles. Stronger and stronger. I seemed to swallow it all.

I choked water as more rushed at me. Bashed me, pressed me down. The pain in my throat, my eyes seeing sky and water alternately. A million bubbles swirling in the green. Then sky, then bubbles . . . I wondered what Mum would say. What they would announce in school.

Arms came under mine, lifted me and pushed me. Fighting with me, forward and back, then forward and I was pushed up the rock face like a slimy lizard.

On it lay Warby. Who then . . . ?

I turned and through frosted eyes saw Dad with the suitcase in his grip. His T-shirt clung to his chest, his face utterly white but for the frightening blue of his eyes.

He was going back the way we had come, staggering through the waves. Each one threw him against the cliff then seemed to suck him back even as he fought his way along the face.

I looked to Warby, who lay like a half-dead fish.

'Where?' I gasped.

Warby pointed to the bay we were making for. Dad had been coming the other way on us. He must've got a taxi along the cliff top.

I watched him battling. Making slow headway. Then from the rock two men appeared. They were glazed and out of focus but I knew who they must be. Dad stopped and so did they. Both surprised by the other.

Dad turned, they clambered down the rock.

Dad fought his way in madness now back to us, the case on his shoulders. He seemed to plough through all that the sea could throw at him. Then Eddie, I could make him out now, arm against the cliff and Spots immediately after, like hounds after a hare.

Eddie was shouting but the sound was lost. It was like a slow motion race; the water slowed them frame by frame.

Spots dropped back then stopped, supported himself against the cliff gasping. Dad had reached the rock where we were, and began to feel for handholds, his hands grasping and moving, his eyes appealing.

Then Eddie was on him and they began to wrestle in the surf. The suitcase fell and both struggled for it pulled back by the other. Now they bundled over and

177

over in the waves, first one on top then the other. Then lost in the sea. Then Dad was up and pounding at Eddie lying in the surf.

Dad tore away. He lifted the case even as Eddie grasped him round the waist. Dad drew him along to the rock and tossed the case onto the rock before collapsing in Eddie's arms.

The case lay near me. I let it be. Spots was making his way to us hand over hand along the cliff. Eddie was no longer interested in Dad who was trying feebly to climb the rock.

Spots drew up and lifted Eddie onto the rock. Warby suddenly rose and took up the case and backed sea-wards as Eddie scrambled to his feet.

'Gimme it, kid.'

Warby reached the end of the rock, ten foot above white water. He turned and waited for Eddie who came for him, slowly like a tag wrestler.

I got up – what to do I don't know, and followed Eddie, who was coming at Warby arms wide. Warby feigned this way and that. Eddie came straight and slow. I was right behind.

At Warby's back the spray rushed and hissed. He stood drenched, suitcase in his hand, tired, afraid and brave as anyone I ever saw. Eddie came on. Warby stood and stupidly challenged him.

Eddie thrust out an arm and pushed up Warby's chin and jerked the suitcase down. It pulled from his hand.

I crouched down and Warby rushed at Eddie. Eddie fell back over me. The case dropped from his hand, slammed on the rock, bounced over the edge, struck a spear of rock and split open like a butterfly on an arch of water.

When the wave died the suitcase lay face down in the water. Scattered about it like tiny boats visiting a liner were the bobbing packets of money.

30

All of us were on the rock, Dad, Spots, Eddie, Warby and myself, watching the break-up of our fortune. With each wave there was ten thousand less.

Dad sat on the side, where the money had gone over, staring – as if he thought with enough concentration he could do a rewind. The waves beat up and sprayed him. He was drenched, his skin pale blue. I was afraid for him; I thought he might jump.

Eddie and Spots stood above him hypnotized by the same sight. With each wave you could see their pain. Spots swearing over and over, Eddie wincing like he was having a hundred injection shots.

Warby and I huddled together. Warby had given me his shirt but we were both soaked through. I was goose pimply, my teeth chattered, worn out. I wanted hot soup, gallons of hot soup, blankets, piles of blankets, sleep, years of it. Warby shivered beside me, shaking me as he shook.

I shall always remember my time on that rock. We were numbed. Not a word spoken between us. It was like we were posing for a picture. Someone was drawing us, they had given us our stories. They said, 'Don't move. And watch the money go.'

The money had taken us all. We had believed in what it could offer us. Me and Dad were the worse cases. Warby wanted lots of money to buy a zoo. Money can do that. It can buy things. Me and Dad wanted the money to change ourselves.

Watching Dad I felt strange. It was as if he were at the graveside of a dead child. His only child, that he loved beyond anything. Hadn't he told me how much he could love. There he was proving it.

Brazil was a lie. We might go there but it was a lie. It would not be a different life. Dad rich or poor was still Dad and Dad would betray me like he always betrayed Mum.

Maybe he'd always come back with presents but your heart can't break that many times. I would hate him in the end.

He sat now huddled and dripping. Small and lost. In some ways younger than me.

I learnt too much on that rock. About me, about my dad. I was stuck with myself. That's what I learnt most of all. Whether I sat in Buckingham Palace or laid out on a park bench – Shorty was Shorty. That was the basic stuff.

Dad still thought he could change it with a pile of money. I want to shake him now, to get it into his head. 'Dad! If you can't love without it you won't love with it.'

He was the first to go. Hours and hours had gone by with nothing seeming to change. But it had. In me and in the sea. It was now drawing back from its high water mark.

Dad jumped into the water by the cliff. It was up to his chest. The sea smashed at him as he made his way along the face, not turning. He would disappear in the waves and then we would see him a little further on; a head and two arms battling. He finally made it to the next rocks, climbed them and disappeared.

Spots and Eddie left sometime after and then me and Warby.

That was all a year ago now. In some ways it seems much more and in some ways no time at all. I only have to close my eyes to see the waves washing Dad as he watched the packets of money bobbing in the sea.

Mum was cut up about the whole business. She'd had the police out when we didn't come back that first day. She got the whole story out of me and Kathy. The money, the train journey, the chase, Dad, everything.

When we finished she didn't speak for a long time. I reckon she was shocked but wondering also what to do.

The next day she went into school with us. She saw the headmaster. He had me and Kathy up before him and we went over the details again. Warby was called in and he admitted it. Then his mum and dad were called. Then Sue and her parents came.

They all had a conflab in the headmaster's study while we sat outside. We could hear them all talking at once, going on for about an hour. Then Mr Kershaw came out and told us they were going to call the police.

We must've spent a week talking to the police. We'd

make a statement then go home, then they'd want to see us again. Always one at a time. They'd read out the statement then I'd sign.

They said they were going to charge us. Then it all quietened down for a while until it came up in juvenile court. My ears still burn when I think of that. They really lectured us. How we must've known it was stolen money and we should be ashamed of ourselves and they would have sent us to approved school but for the fact that our parents and teachers spoke up for us.

We all got two years' probation. I have to go and talk to a probation officer once a week. She keeps warning me to keep out of trouble. Which I have done. Besides I'm not into thieving and the chances of finding a suitcase full of money is about as likely as finding planet David.

As for the grown ups the cops wanted to do them but couldn't find a charge. I mean we'd done all the spending except that bit we'd given Eddie in the beginning. He said we were a bunch of liars and that all he was doing was trying to get the money off us to hand over to the law. No one believed that but they slid out of it.

Eddie disappeared a few months back. Warby figures either the gang are after him or the cops want him for something else.

And that I suppose is the end of it really except one day when I came in from school there was Kathy puzzling over this postcard. It was addressed to me but didn't say who it was from.

The message on the back said 'Me and You'. On the front was a picture of Rio de Janeiro.

I suppose he'll be back one day. And I doubt he'll have changed. But I have. I learnt the trick. I learnt to like myself a bit. Not too much – that's just a swelled head – but enough to know that the world hasn't got it in for me. And if I don't make excuses or wait for suitcases of money, there'll be chances to make something of myself. There'll be people who'll like me for what I am.

I learnt I'm alright.